I0670847

ABOUT ROBYN SMYTHE

Robyn Smythe is a Scottish writer. Born in the Sixties in Fife, he was educated at Madras College secondary school where he wrote his first full length story. More than three decades later, after a varied working life that has involved being a lifeguard and Post Office clerk, he finally found time to write Fallon, his debut novel. He is married with two teenage girls and is currently working on a third Fallon novel, *The Gathering Storm*, which will be out in 2024.

Previous titles by the same author

"The Animal Tea Party"

"Fallon – Non Est Optio Defectum"

"Fudge – A Short Tail of Tooth and Claw"

ROBYN SMYTHE
FALLON

The Legacy Series:

Part Two – 'Family Above All'

Grosvenor House
Publishing Limited

This book is published by
Grosvenor House Publishing Ltd
Link House
140 The Broadway, Tolworth, Surrey, KT6 7HT.
www.grosvenorhousepublishing.co.uk

A CIP record for this book
is available from the British Library

ISBN 978-1-80381-693-7

Fallon: Family Above All

This Book is dedicated to David
and Jean, my parents. As I gave
birth to a legend, they gave
birth to me.

All my love.

Rx

Prologue

It was the end of September 1954. Like all the summers after the passing of his beloved wife, Molly-Beth, it had been a mixed bag of emotions for Jonathan Fallon as he sat in his favourite chair looking out of the window. Tinged with sadness over the loss of his soul mate, but this had begun to ebb, like the morning tide, into his memory. The combined idea concocted by his friend Jericho Smithers and his son, Peter, to send his granddaughter to help him get over his grief turned out to be one of inspiration.

Molly was now eleven and like children of her age, she was a firecracker of energy and enthusiasm. She hung on his every word like a necklace would around his neck, listening to his tall stories of daring-do and high adventure touched with a smidgen of nonsense. A prime example of this was 'The Animal Tea Party' which told the silly, but comical story, of a group of animals having a chat whilst eating and drinking. Molly loved it, and it helped her get over her fright she had from the raging storm outside. He would eventually take her back to bed and then sit in his office, or study as it was labelled on the blueprints of the Manor, and let his mind drift off to how his beloved and him met. Goodness, it was hard to believe that was almost a year ago since he had buried her.

Fallon looked across at his glass of whisky. Should he take another sip from this regal of all drinks. He was already feeling the effects from the last couple or was it the sheer exhaustion brought on by that ball of red headed mischief that was Molly Fallon? Whatever had caused it, the feeling had secretly crept up on him and he could feel his eyes beginning to succumb to its mystical powers. To begin with, he fought against it. Shaking himself back to consciousness. Twice he had won the battle but the third time, the mixture of fatigue and alcohol was too much to bear, and his eyelids met as he fell into a deep sleep. His mind began to rewind the clock back to happier times as a strange sound came from his mouth – a snore.

1 – Memories

It was the 11th of July 1920 and Jonathan Fallon married Molly-Beth Ashton in front of family and friends. It was a joyous affair, with everyone trying their hardest to forget the hardship and trauma of the Great War that had ended only a few years before. But a spectre from Fallon's past would rear his ugly head – Johannes Riga.

It was five in the morning when Fallon appeared at the top of the staircase and quietly tip-toed downstairs. He tried a few doors before finding the drawing room, and went in. There was a table at the back of the room, and after much fumbling, cursing and even stubbing his toe on the desk, he found a light switch and clicked it on. The light from the reading lamp barely lit about three feet in front of the desk, but it was enough for him to find his pipe, and after a short rummage, his box of matches. He was about to strike one of the matches when he noticed a beautifully wrapped box in the middle of the desk. He pulled it round so he could read the label: 'To J love always MB xx'.

1

He carefully unwrapped the box, and found a silver plated lighter in the shape of an automatic, the kind a lady would carry in her clutch bag. On the lighter was engraved a shield with a capital 'F' on it, and a scroll with the legend 'Non Est Optio Defectum.'

"Failure is not an Option." Fallon said, thanking the head of the Office of Special Projects, Colonel John Forrester, who had drummed this phrase religiously into his head since he joined the unit.

"But you have failed, Herr Fallon!" Corrected a heavily accented voice from across the room. Fallon spun round to face the source of the voice and saw a man standing their wearing a black ankle length leather coat, a fedora hat, and dark boots. A Luger pistol pointed at Fallon's chest. Fallon squinted to try and focus. The stranger walked into the semi-circle of light given off by the desk lamp. The arrival's face was heavily scarred, and he walked with the aid of a cane.

"Riga!" Fallon said horrified.

"I see you recognise me, Mein Herr." He clicked his heels together and gave a short bow of his head. "Sit down please with your hands where I can see them." He motioned to the chair behind the desk with his pistol.

"I see the years haven't been kind to you."

"Ach. The scars of the young, Mein Herr. After our little adventure in Egypt, I managed to get back to the Fatherland via many modes of transport from ships to planes and even a train at one point. It was whilst I was on one of the ships, a cheap, stinking steamer, that it was torpedoed by one of your submarines and I was

2

lucky to escape with my life, but I have these memories," he touched the scars with the back of his pistol as he moved over to sit in a chair facing Fallon, "to aid in my revenge."

"Our little adventure? You tried to kill several very important Egyptian officials and start an African Front..."

"Ach.... but that is the past. I see you have done well for yourself." He used the pistol to point to the room they were in, signifying the whole house, "and you have just married the delightful Miss Ashton or should I say Mrs Fallon..."

"What do you want, Riga?"

"I want.... YOU." He pointed the Luger square at Fallon's chest. Fallon braced himself. "You cost me everything. My titles back home. My family disowned me. Even my benefactors in the German military treat me like judas." Fallon shrugged his shoulders which only stoked Riga's fury. He jumped to his feet causing the chair to fall with a crash. His hand holding the pistol was shaking so much that he had to drop his cane and use his other hand to steady it. "You DARE shrug your shoulders at me like some pompous devil may care!" He spat screaming at the top of his voice. Fallon's eyes were wide. Searching his surroundings for an aid, something he could use to defend himself. Just then, the drawing room door creaked open, and a woman's hand appeared around the door.

"Darling, are you all, right? I heard something fall and thought you might have..." Molly stopped in mid-sentence as she came face to face with Riga. He raised his

3

gun to fire. Molly let out a scream and closed her eyes, but the kill-shot never came. Clunk. The pistol fell from Riga's hand and a trickle of red blood appeared at the side of his mouth. He let out a strangled last gasp before hitting the floor face down, a letter opener buried deep in his back, the one that Fallon had thrown from across the room. Fallon came round the desk just in time to catch his wife who rushed into his arms sobbing.

"Well. He got the point." Fallon said, looking down at the lifeless body on the floor before burying his face in the neck of his wife.

The first person Fallon called after Molly had calmed down was his boss, Colonel Forrester. Once he had explained what had happened, Forrester said not to worry and to take Molly away somewhere nice for a couple of days and he would sort everything out.

The newly-weds jumped into Fallon's battered old car and drove most of the morning across the border into Scotland. Typical Scottish weather, sunshine in England but as soon as they crossed the border, it began to pelt it down with rain. So heavy was the downpour that the windscreen wipers were struggling to cope. They drove as far as they could before managing to find one of those quaint roadside hotels that seem to pop up as if by magic. They pulled in and ran inside.

The smell of whisky caught their nostrils as they opened the front door of the hotel – The Capercaillie. Named after one of the wild breeds of birds that inhabit the Highlands, I believe. The reception area doubled as the bar and Fallon looked around, surprised to see a couple of old men seated

4

at the bar with a small glass of the amber nectar. Each lifted their glasses at the newcomers before returning to their conversation. Fallon rang the bell on top of the bar and an old woman shuffled out from another part of the bar.

"Ah. How can I help ye?" She asked. Her voice had a kind of soothing lilt to it.

"A room please."

"For two?" Fallon nodded. "We have one with a double bed. Would that be satisfactory?"

"That would be perfect." Replied Fallon looking over to Molly and gazing into her eyes.

"Would ya be newly-weds?" Enquired the old woman with a large grin on her face.

"Aye, we would."

"Och, that's braw!" She took out the register book from beneath the bar and plonked it on top, opening it at the marked page, and placing a pen on it. "I've got the Fleming suite for you. Number seven. Just up the stairs and to your right."

"Thank you." Said Fallon signing his name. The old woman handed him a key attached to a small wooden fob with the number seven inked on it.

"How long are you staying for?" She asked as they started to climb the stairs.

"Not sure." Came the reply.

"Och, ain't that bonnie." She said using her right hand to swat an imaginary fly and then disappeared around the corner.

They stopped outside number seven, Fallon turned the key and the door opened revealing a small room with a tiny wardrobe to the left, a double bed with one side table and a small window to the right. The curtains were already closed.

"How many children do you want, Mister Fallon?"

"I don't know, Missus Fallon? How many do you want?"

"Three." They kissed. "Four." They kissed again. "Five." The door closed. "Failure is not an Option...."

2 – Settled

Married life suited the Fallons but C.J Ashton, Molly-Beth's father, sadly died unexpectantly of a heart attack three months after his daughter's marriage. This made Molly-Beth re-evaluate her life and, with her husband's blessing, she resigned from the Office of Special Projects and went back to university gaining a degree in teaching, however, Forrester managed to lure her back, creating a new post for her, making use of her new degree as a cover story.

Fallon continued to work for the OSP as a field operative and Molly was a training officer in charge of linguistics or languages. Her cover story was that she was teaching in the Capital which helped explain about her travelling and her absence from the Estate.

The Ashton estate, including Ashton Manor, was left in the capable hands of Jericho Smithers after he was invalided out of the OSP due to the injuries sustained in the Riga Affair. He would function as both manager and manservant. Smithers took to the new role like a duck to

7

water, maintaining the order in his life he was used to in the services. He ran a tight ship drafting schedules for the rest of the staff which consisted of a gardener and a chauffeur.

Fallon had returned from an assignment at the end of August to find the gardener hard at work tending the two very large gardens, one at the front of the house and one at the back, especially the several rose bushes, they were his passion. The gardener, as it turned out, was an old Army buddy of Smithers who had been invalided out with shell shock or post-traumatic stress disorder, to give it its more modern name. Jenkins was his name. The chauffeur, too, was a *'friend'* of Smithers but not from his army days, but before he enlisted. His name was Baldwin and had a shadier past, something he would shy away from talking about, but Smithers swore by him.

"He knows how to manage and maintain a car, Sir." Would have been his reply if Fallon pushed him on the matter. Another former soldier joined the staff on the estate – Archie 'Nails' O'Hanlon. He just appeared on the doorstep of the manor asking for a job one evening. Because of his military background, Fallon hired him as the estate's gamekeeper and allowed him to assume residence in the small cottage by the lake.

That August was a warm affair. The weather was hot and steamy, the night's too. Molly-Beth like to show her husband how much she missed him when he returned from a mission, but she never pressed him about the details, as she understood he was not allowed to discuss anything. The pair would rise early and take walks in the

8

woods adjacent to the manor, hand in hand, arms swinging and smiles on their fresh faces. They had two routes to choose from as they stood at the end of the driveway – to their left was the road that led them to Brave Acre village.

Originally built to house the labourers that worked on the surrounding farms, it had sprouted into a nice little hamlet with its own church, St Robert's of the Angel with the Broken Wing, where the Reverend Damien Pimpelhorn resided next door in the manse with his family; a pub called '*The Cat in the Boot*,' ably run by Jeannie Mackie; there was even a school to educate the children, which was teacherless at the moment. There was a small shop that catered for everything, run by '*Nana*' Elsie Swinton. If she did not have what you needed, give her a few hours and it would miraculously appear on the shelf, as if it had been there all along, or she would have it behind the counter with your name on it. It was rumoured that '*Nana*' had dealings with the black market, but no one dared to say this in public.

A small one man police station was there too, home to Constable Desmond '*Des*' Hawkins who patrolled the local area on his trusty bicycle complete with basket on the front. At the centre of the village was the square, which contained a large circular fountain, bus stop, and a war memorial commemorating the fallen in past conflicts. There was a small square building that was affectionately referred to as 'The Village Hall.' This was where the summer farmers dances were held, allowing people from the surrounding area to let their hair down and have a good time.

9

On their right, the road led them to the start of what they called 'the circle.' It consisted of a walk that took them into the countryside heading towards a local farm they both knew well, that sold fresh strawberries. Depending upon the time of day, they would sometimes stop there, buy a punnet or two and eat them as they walked. From the farm, you turned right along a farm track, and this took you through a small, wooded area, through another farm consisting of a farmhouse, a couple of barns and a broken down tractor parked out the front of the farmhouse, and then on to a dirt track, which opened out on to a wonderful view of Golf City with its cathedral ruins and thirty-three metre (108 feet) tall square tower left over from a bye-gone age.

It was a university town and the red gowned rich kids let you know it directly with their shouting and hollering at all times of the day and night. Several times, Smithers had contacted the police to complain about broken fences around the estate, witnessing the outright vandalism himself, only to be told by a desk sergeant that they would put it down to a student prank. One of the local boys broke a streetlamp, true it was in front of a policeman, and he was charged and ordered to pay for the repairs. The student that broke the fence did not get away scot-free either. He was found lying face down in an alley a few days later swearing blind that he was attacked by a man who smelt of roses.

The fields on their walk were like a gigantic patchwork quilt of browns, yellows, and greens. Some had cereal crops in them, others grass, and some had vegetables.

The rich musky odour of farm animals mixed with the smell of life and growing. There was a couple of houses at the top of the walk, lovely view in the Summer but it must be hellish in the Winter when the snow comes. A couple of cows mooed a low mellow greeting as the couple walked past. Molly-Beth squeezed Fallon's hand and he put his arm around her, her arm slipped around his waist like a boa-constrictor would its prey. They walked like this, joined at the hip, down the other side of the hill, past some men making hay with a horse drawn harvester.

One of the men waved. It was 'Big' Cyril Musgrave. He was the owner of the second farm, the one with the broken tractor. Molly-Beth said that Cyril always kept saying that he was going to get around to fixing that damn tractor someday but to this date, he never has. The two waved back. A couple riding horses made them stop in their tracks. The animals seemed to appear as if by magic. One of the riders, a large woman with buck teeth and a riding jacket whose buttons were straining under the task of keeping her bulk under wraps, said something haughty with a mixture of grunts and snorts before using a whisk of her whip on her mounts side to spurn it on to catch up with her friend.

They were on the main road now and had to move on to the grass verge a few times as the odd car would trundle past. On their left, was a caravan park and they decided to cut through it, using it as a short cut. The caravans were large tin affairs and going by the amount of grass growing underneath each one, they had been there for a while. Most were holiday homes before the war but had run into disrepair after the owners failed to return. Some for financial reasons. Others just failed to return home, period. It was a stark reminder of the cost of the conflict. Very few families were not touched by the evil hand of war.

The politicians playing real life monopoly with people's lives instead of metal pieces. That was what his father used to say every time Fallon came home from leave from the front. His father Struan had served in the diplomatic service before the war and had warned his superiors on several occasions what a powder keg the Balkans were becoming but nobody listened. It was one of those 'I told you so' moments but at what cost? Suddenly, Molly-Beth let out a loud laugh that snapped Fallon back to the present.

"What the hell?" He asked as his wife pointed to a large stuffed rabbit in the glass doorway of one of the caravans. Fallon shook his head and smiled at his wife's quirkiness. He liked it when she smiled or laughed as the freckles across her nose seemed to join up, her red hair glinted in the sunlight, like hot lava cascading down a hillside. He stopped and looked at her, transfixed by her beauty. His silence made her stop laughing and they stood looking at each other, eyes locked as if trapped in a quagmire of love.

"Here, will you two love birds wanna get a shifty on!"

Their gaze was broken, and they turned around to see who was speaking. It was Cyril. He reminded Fallon of a picture he had seen as a child of a caricature of how humpty-dumpty would look like from the nursery rhyme, complete with egg shaped body, round eyes, and stumpy legs. To top it off, Cyril had a tweed waistcoat on and a flat grandad cap on his head, protecting the last remnants of hair he had left. He sat in the driver's seat of a small two-person cart with two large wheels and was being pulled by a big Shire horse called 'Bert,' who was partial to carrots, but only when Cyril was not looking. His pride and joy, like a Captain with his ship.

Bert whinnied as Fallon and Molly-Beth moved out of the way allowing the cart by. Cyril touched his cap with his right index finger before flicking the reins making Bert quicken his pace. "Will I be seeing you at the Drowned Neighbours tonight?" Shouted Cyril as he disappeared over the hill. The 'Drowned Neighbours' was the name of one of the public houses in the town. The local for the Fallon's and most of the surrounding farm folk.

The locals tended to stay away from the centre of town because that was 'student' country. Over the past few months, a few of the local lads had ventured into 'student' country wanting to sample some of the high life, only to end up with a night in the cells after a brawl with a group of academics. Fallon looked at his watch. It was three in the afternoon. Three thirty by the time they made it back to the manor. Smithers was waiting for them on the stairs as their feet scrunched under the stones that covered the driveway.

"The mail has arrived, Sir and a telephone call from the Colonel. He asks you to call him back at your earliest convenience." The Colonel, Smithers was referring to was Colonel John Forrester.

"Thank you." He took the four envelopes from Smithers, and they went inside. Fallon picked up the telephone, which was on a small table just inside the door and called his boss. After several redirections and going through a barrage of security checks, his boss' gruff voice could be heard on the line.

"Forrester."

"Fallon, Sir."

"Ah, K-twelve. Thanks for calling me back. I was calling to let you know that we have been given orders to stand down and await further orders."

"But why, Sir? I still haven't found who was financing Riga's Egyptian operation."

"Orders, K-twelve. We've been investigating this case for almost two years and produced nothing. Because of this, the powers-that-be have pulled the plug."

"But Sir!" Fallon protested.

"But nothing, K-twelve!" Snapped Forrester, "enjoy married life. Rest. Recuperate. That's an order." The phone went dead.

"Damnit!" Fallon cursed as he threw the phone down so hard that he almost knocked the whole thing off the table.

3 – A New Addition

The evening air had a bite to it. A chill. Molly-Beth pulled her shawl tightly around her shoulders as they walked down towards the outskirts of town. The road was deserted. Sheep and cows went about their business in the fields flanking the road. Eating, sleeping, and adding to the enrichment of the soil. The leaves above them rustled in the gentle breeze. There was a definite change in the air. The Fallons walked slowly hand in hand. There was no rush. They were enjoying both their company and the surroundings. A bird rose from the hedgerow up ahead. Something had startled it. The Fallons stopped and looked up ahead in time to see a fox dart out from beneath the hedgerow. Its copper like coat moving as each muscle beneath flexed and relaxed as it moved. Its tail perfect counterbalance to its body. The white tip moving up and down as the animal crossed the road while its ears constantly flicked scanning for any sounds of either prey or danger. It disappeared as quickly as it had appeared.

A sign creaked backwards and forwards above their heads as the Fallons stopped outside the public house. 'The Drowned Neighbours' had a ghoulish picture painted on said sign. It showed two men holding another man's head under the water with the two men looking straight out at you from the sign and smiling. Over the years, there had been many complaints and requests for the owners to change the sign or the name of the pub, but each suggestion was met by the same response. It added to the charm of the building. It was a talking point. People came to complain or comment and ended up having something to eat and a pint of something cold. Why spoil a good thing?

Anyway, the pub was a rarity these days – a family-owned affair and not under the umbrella of some unseen brewery bully. Sam and Joyce Watson were the current owners. Sam was the chef and Joyce the barmaid. Both were local and well known in the town. Both made you feel welcome when you entered and made sure you got home okay after you had sampled some of their produce whether of the gourmet or liquid variety. Fallon pulled open the front door, ushered Molly-Beth in before going in, allowing the door to hit him gently on the rear. Big Cyril was up at the far end of the bar and waved. His booming voice unmistakable as was his rather large frame, hence his nickname.

"I'll be buying the Fallons a drink, Joyce." He announced pulling out his wallet from the inside of his waistcoat. Joyce's hand hovered over one of the three beer taps that stuck up in front of her. One was a local brew; one was some imported swill, and the other was a well-known brand.

"Thanks Cyril. I'll have some of the Foxglove." Fallon pointed to the local brew. The local brew had a reputation of being nice when you first tasted it but smacking you in the mouth like a heavyweight boxer once it touched the back of your throat. To most, it was an acquired taste.

"Just some tonic for me please." Replied Molly-Beth sitting down on one of the numerous stools parked in front of the bar. Joyce looked at Fallon as if for confirmation. Fallon nodded. She poured the local brew expertly into a pint glass. Its tanned body topped off with just enough white froth. There was a fizzing sound as Joyce opened a bottle of tonic water and poured it into a clean glass before placing it in front of Molly-Beth. Now, Joyce was not a small woman by any sense of the word but as soon as money was involved, she could have a turn of speed. It looked like someone had pressed the turbo boost button as she zeroed in on Cyril's outstretched hand like a falcon diving down on an unsuspecting rabbit in one of the fields. Snap and his notes were gone into the register to be replaced by the chink-chink-chink of coins.

A momentary look of disappointment appeared on his face as he looked down at the metal circles in his hand, but this was soon replaced by his usual guffawing laugh as he slapped some unsuspecting man next to him on the back, nearly making the man spill his drink. The bar murmured with conversation like a highly tuned engine. Laughter. Shouting. All mixed with the cigarette and pipe smoke that hung just above them like an ozone layer

1 7

between them and the ceiling. The topics of conversation? Who cares! People were there to chew the fat and enjoy themselves a one and others company.

The moon had come up by the time the Fallons made their weary way back towards the manor house. Fallon was swaying a little, the Foxglove was a potent flower in real life and just as unfriendly in liquid form. Molly-Beth walked beside him, sometimes correcting his direction but did so without saying a word. His usual talkative wife was strangely quiet, thoughtfully quiet, and this bothered Fallon. He stopped when they reached the beginning of their driveway and turned to look at her square in the face. Admittedly, it did take him a few minutes to focus.

"What's wrong?" He asked. She looked at him and gave a contented smile. He took both her hands in his. "Is it something I've done?" A worried tone crept into his voice.

"You could say that." There was that bloody contented smile again.

"Oh. I am sorry." He said sheepishly dropping her hands. "Whatever I have done, I promise I won't do it again." Fallon went on the defensive. They had not been married very long but he had already learned that cowardice was the best policy and defence mechanism when it came to his wife.

"Too late. The damage is done." She smiled again and started to walk up the drive, her feet crunching on the stones and on her husband's senses. He started to run after her but lost his footing and went face first on to the ground. His wife stopped and laughed as he lay there, his pride hurt more than anything else. Instead of getting back up, he pulled himself up into a sitting position with his legs splayed out front.

"What have I done?" He asked again.

"Darling Johnny..." She began as she came back and kneeled in front of him and she took hold of his hands, looking him square in the eye. "I'm pregnant." Inside Fallon's head, it took a while for that statement to process. Like someone had entered a darkened room and had just found the light switch. Click and the bulb, high in the ceiling, had gone on.

"Your ppp..." He stuttered. I told you the light bulb was quite high up and not illuminating very much.

"Pregnant." She finished.

"How? When? Who's is it?" Were the only words that tumbled from his mouth, like a stone rolling down the side of a hill of stupidity. This seems to be the standard reply given by partners who find out that the world as they know it will change forever in approximately nine months, give, or take. In response – Molly-Beth just glared and then helped him slowly to his feet. But instantly, another switch was flicked in Fallon's brain, that of protector. He quickly brushed off her assistance and wrapped his arm around her, shepherding her gently up the drive towards the house. Fussing over her like a mother hen. Making sure each foot fall was planted properly. He almost sobered up there on the spot.

As Summer made way for Autumn and the leaves in the trees turned from shades of green to shades of brown, and gold becoming crisp under foot, the crops in the fields gave way to emptiness, that could not be said about Molly-Beth, who's tummy began to swell, and a glow fell upon her skin. A reverence that women seem to get when they are with child. It was not long before the close-knit community in town found out too and started to treat Molly-Beth differently. If you pardon the pun, with kid-gloves.

The women in her reading circle, a group of busy bodies that set the town to rights when they were discussing some trashy novel, told her to sit down while they fussed around her making cups of dishwater thin tea and terrible sandwiches, the ingredients of which even make this writer's stomach turn, so I won't endanger you by committing them to print. Like the reading group, the knitting group was held once a week at the manor house.

Molly-Beth was the youngest one there and it was made up of mostly middle-aged women whose husbands had either turfed them out for the afternoon so they could get some peace and quiet, so they could go to the pub or were playing crown green bowls down at the bowling club beside the river. The knitters had started clicking and clacking their needles making booties and little tops or bonnets for the baby. Fallon even accepted bowls to escape the continual nattering and click/clacking. He was not very good. Give him a Lee Enfield rifle and a fly's crown jewels would be in jeopardy of being shot off but try placing a bowl within a certain distance on an ironing board flat piece of grass, and that was something completely different.

Winter. Christmas that year was a joyous affair but touched with a tinge of sadness. Molly-Beth remembered her late father and raised a glass of orange juice to his memory. Fallon had managed to procure a tree from the forest, ably assisted by Smithers and Cyril. The decorations and tinsel shimmered in the light from the log fire that was burning in the hearth. Carol singers came to the door and sang their hearts out. Several were so out of tune, Fallon pleaded with Molly-Beth to allow him to get his rifle and put them out of their misery, but she refused the request. They had family over.

Struan and Isabella, Fallon's parents came up from Wales, Stephanie, Molly-Beth's mother, popped over from France where she had moved to after C.J had passed. Cyril and his family popped in too which added to Smithers already hectic workload. A turkey was bought and cooked with all the trimmings. Various beverages were opened and consumed. Because the villagers had been suffering due to the financial climate, the Fallons had opened their doors to them and this in turn, swelled the ranks of those gathered to celebrate the festivities and went along way to cementing friendships and tightening bonds. A good time was had by all.

When the snow came, it hit hard. Deep drifts and perishing icy winds made Cyril's job an uphill struggle. Fallon and several of the men from town were drafted in rescuing sheep and dealing with fallen trees. The latter was used on various fireplaces within the town. The snow carpeted the land in a thick, deep watery whiteness that made everyone wrap up warm and only venture out when it was needed. Fallon was glad the manor house was big and had several rooms that allowed his festive guests to stay longer than was planned. Each apologising for the inconvenience and each told that it was no bother.

Spring. The weather starts to warm up and the promise of new life. The snow becomes a distant memory as new grass appears. Young farm animals add their own voices to the air. Lambs and calves jump and ran in the fields. Even old Bert, Cyril's trusted Shire horse, sowed his oats and became a father again, much to the surprise of his owner.

"By Golly!" Said a stunned but proud Cyril, "I did nae think the old fella could still do it."

That was another wetting the baby's, or foal's, head party that Fallon staggered home from one night at the end of March. Molly-Beth used to be bothered by her husband's drinking but soon realised, with the devil that is drink, served two vital purposes – the first being, it cemented their relationships with the wider community, most of whom had become their dear friends. The second, it allowed Fallon to unwind after a mission. No-one outside those who lived and worked at the Manor house knew exactly what he did. Not even their extended family. For them, and the others that came into their orbit, Fallon just worked for the Government as a trouble-shooter, a term coined by her late father, which could not be closer to the truth that if you had hit the proverbial nail on the head. Some suit in Westminster, was how Big Cyril once described his mysterious friend to a passer-by in the pub one night.

It took him at least three attempts to climb the three steps to the main door. The steps, certainly from his perception, had grown in height in the time it had taken him to go to the pub and back again. He could be heard clattering around downstairs and telling himself to be quiet. A strange 'shooshing' sound could be heard coming from his mouth as well as another gobble-dee-gook that even Molly-Beth could not understand.

Have you ever noticed, that, when people are drunk or have had way too much to drink, they suddenly become comedians. In their pickled minds, they are the funniest person alive even laughing at a joke that has not been uttered aloud. His movement was elongated. His steps long and purposeful. Each footfall carefully thought out and then accompanied by manic giggling. He staggered and then propped himself up against the wall. Staggered and propped. Propped and staggered like he was choreographing the moves of weird Latin dance that only he knew the steps for. He looked like a mannequin whose strings had just been cut, the way he was flopping around about the place.

This strange movement did, however, manage to get him into his intended destination – his study. He dove for the couch performing a feat of elegance that an Olympic diver would score high execution marks on, and then there was silence. Well, not really if you counted the alcohol fuelled snoring. Tuneful but extremely annoying.

The following morning, Molly-Beth and Smithers conspired together to wreck vengeance upon him by cooking up the greasiest breakfast one could imagine.

2 3

Runny eggs, tomatoes fried within an inch of their red skinned lives, bacon with the fat still on, black pudding that was blacker than night, toast beaten into submission all washed down with the strongest coffee Smithers could muster. He diligently warned all assembled not to spill the black tar-like substance on the table, otherwise they would have to get it revarnished. A warning noted by all, and a groan from Fallon, who cradled his throbbing brow in both hands.

April 10th, 1921. A date that will live in infamy (a phrase that will be used some twenty years later by President Theodore Roosevelt to describe the Japanese sneak attack on Pearl Harbour). It began in the early hours by Molly-Beth screaming the house down. Fallon had been downstairs in his study going over some mission reports. When the screaming started, the once orderly pile of papers erupted into a tornado, as Fallon sprinted to his wife's side. Smithers was up, as was Jenkins, the gardener, and Baldwin the chauffeur. It was time. Smithers did what Smithers always did, swung their well drilled plan into operation.

Baldwin was dressed and out warming up the car before you could say 'Baldwin...' whilst Jenkins was telephoning the hospital which was some ten minutes the other side of the town. Smithers went upstairs and started bossing Fallon around, who was beside himself, telling him to get dressed and allow Smithers to deal with Molly-Beth. It amazed Smithers how calm and collected Fallon could be whilst under-fire but put him in a situation where his wife was about to have a baby, well,

2 4

that was a different situation, the man turned into a blithering idiot.

"The car is ready, and the hospital are aware." Informed Jenkins from the bedroom door. He skipped around and assisted Molly-Beth to her feet who was breathing heavy. Fallon caught the bag that Smithers threw at him, and the group slowly and carefully made their way down the stairs and out to the awaiting car.

Molly-Beth went in the back. Fallon was bundled in beside her and Smithers got into the front passenger seat, with Baldwin driving. Down the gravel track they sped, then a sharp left. A moan came from the back seat causing Baldwin to apologise. Through the deserted streets. Another left turn, another apology. Along what the locals called 'The Drive' which was a straight road that measured exactly one mile in length. A left turn. An apology and there, was the hospital up on the left all lit up like a Christmas tree.

They came to a screeching halt. Another apology. The main doors of the hospital were flung open and out strode a fearsome looking matron. The rear passenger door opened, and Molly-Beth was prized out of the vehicle like you would a sardine from the can. A white coated orderly appeared with a wheelchair and Molly-Beth was plonked into it and wheeled off. The three men climbed out of the car and began to follow, only to be stopped by the matron. She reminded the ex-military men of a Sergeant Major they had during basic training, complete with moustache that wiggled like a caterpillar amid its death throws as she uttered her commands.

Her dark blue uniform starched with razor sharp creases, lethal enough to kill an unsuspecting father at twenty paces, the men deduced. Her large tree trunk sized arms, folded one over the other, made an impenetrable barrier, blocking further movement like a dam built by an over industrious fifteen stone beaver with a moustache.

"Only the father of the child from here on." Barked the Matron. Smithers tried to get passed her only to be blocked by twin bosoms of steel and a snort of disapproval. He knew when he was fighting a losing battle and raised his hands in surrender, stepping back and sitting down on one of the metal chairs that lined the corridor.

Molly-Beth entered the hospital at 0420. Peter Robert Fallon came into the world at 1924 hours weighing eight pounds two ounces. According to Fallon, the first thing the saw of his son was the top of his head which was covered in red hair.

"How did a snooker ball get there?" Was what he said he thought, as he recounted the birth over a pint at the Drowned Neighbours, a few days later. Molly-Beth and Peter stayed in hospital for a further couple of days under observation just as a precaution, allowing Fallon and his minions to prepare the nursery. They had decided, Molly-Beth and Fallon, but more Molly-Beth, that a neutral colour would go on the walls. Various pictures were hung, and colourful wind-chimes dangled. Drawers began to overflow with clothes both bought by the new parents and given by well-wishers. Advice for the couple flowed like a torrent. Their heads were at bursting point by the time they came home.

A stuffed horse was in the cot, curtesy of Cyril, and the mantelpiece above the fire was covered with cards. Molly-Beth made a mental note, to get round to reading them when she had time. It brought a warm feeling to her knowing that so many people cared. She laid her bundle of joy down in his cot and stood looking at him as he lay there looking back at her. Fallon joined her and put his arm around her waist. Their life had changed for the second time – the first being, when they first met in that bazaar in Cairo, what now seemed like a lifetime ago.

Being parents can test any relationship. The early morning feeds. The nappy changes which vary in degrees of grossness from simple ejections to full blown up the back chicken korma. A strong will is needed as is a strong stomach. The lack of sleep when your child is ill or teething. The screaming and the tantrums both from your offspring and from the parents. One good thing was that financially, they were secure both from the fact that Mary-Beth's family were well-off, and that Fallon's job paid very well. The downside was that, jobwise, Fallon was having to return to work. Deep down, Molly-Beth understood this but emotionally it did cause several arguments that ended up with one or both storming either out of the room or out of the manor.

The latter was usually Fallon, who would cool off by jogging around the grounds. He would stop at the small lake on the property and sit on the bank just gazing out into the water. He would often go for a swim in its cool refreshing water too, sometimes clothed other times not. The hard times though, were counterbalanced with the good. The long walks they took as a family pushing the pram. One midnight feed, in the gloom of the early hours, a tiny hand reached out and grasped Fallon's pinkie making him look down on a contented face. But the contentment was only fleeting and the Fallons knew that. It ended during a visit to the Drowned Neighbours.

4 – Lukas Falcone

Lukas Falcone looked at his watch as he hung around the lamp post like a bad smell. They were late and that annoyed him. His little band of followers doted on him, obeying every word like the sheep they were. In his own way, Falcone both pitied and despised them in equal measure. His father, Alexandre, had made him come to this back water University because it had a reputation for excellence. Reputation for boredom, he thought, as he lit a cigarette and tossed the match to the ground. He stood watching the flame on the match slowly wither and die, just like his prospects at this god forsaken place. He missed the high society parties and gay abandonment of Paris and Madrid. His father was extremely rich, and the wealth rolled downhill like an avalanche of greenbacks.

He used to love going into restaurants, mention his name in an off-the-cuff way and watch the serving staff scurry around like insects, to get a table ready for him and his guests. Now, he must resign himself to bistros and non-descript cafes. Did you know that a member of some royal family met his future bride in one of those unmentionable places? Whoopee! Someone get him a gun so that he can end his miserable existence now. He took a long drag on his cigarette and flicked his fringe of blonde hair out of his eyes just as a group came round the corner of the street. They were laughing and shouting, a couple of them tried to drink from wine bottles as they walked, a hopeless task, which ended up the liquid spilling either on to their clothes or onto the road, which brought more hilarity. They were all in their early twenties, much like Lukas, and were studying a wide variety of courses at the University. Some were super intelligent whilst others scraped along on a wing and a prayer.

"What the bloody hell?" Lukas tapping his watch as they approached. The joyfulness died like the flame on the match. They all looked at him and then bowed their heads in submission before bursting into a cacophony of noise as each tried to blame the others for their tardiness. Lukas raised a hand to silence the noise. "Forget that! I am out to party and nothing's gonna stop us having some fun!" He proclaimed and this raised the volume of celebration to an ear-splitting level. Lukas had spent the morning listening to some old man of a professor withering on about something or someone relevant to his course but all he heard was BLAH! BLAH! BLAH! He had escaped this monotony and wanted to have fun.

He grabbed one of the bottles and took a swig instantly spitting out the pig swill. He looked around the group to see anyone would own up to buying such a vinegar tasting vulgarity, but no-one dared. The bottle broke into a zillion pieces as it hit the pavement. A woman walking by, looked across with a disapproving look but did not stop as Lukas opened his arms as if he were on the cross begging someone to chastise him. The whole group laughed manically before they began their assault on the town's bars. It was noon and already a couple of the group were worse for wear. They used each other as leaning posts, as they tried to stay upright as they tottered after Falcone, who strode ahead like a general leading his troops into battle.

The Drowned Dog was their first port of call. The place was dead and had had about as much atmosphere as a morgue. They stayed for a couple of whiskies before moving on. The Arch. The Regal and the Criterion all benefited from their patronage as their manner began to dive into drunkenness. The once coherent rush of conversation descending into a babble of rubbishness.

An interpreter for the language they began to speak has yet to be found but amazingly, each member of the group understood what was being said as if it was as crystal clear as a mountain spring. They laughed. Cursed. Laughed some more and even cursed some more. They swayed their way down towards the local marina, on their way there, Lukas picked up a stone and threw it at one of the ornamental streetlights smashing it to smithereens. A local policeman happened to be cycling passed at the time and did log the blatant act of vandalism but put it down in his book as a student prank. That same copper would witness a similar act a week later but this time the perpetrator was a local lad, and he was forced to pay for repairs.

The group walked along the shore, stood watching the boats bobbing up and down. One decided to relieve themselves and urinated all over the deck of a nearby fishing boat. A cackle of laughter rewarded the individual as he struggled to pull up his zipper. Their feet clanked on the metal foot bridge that spanned both sides of the harbour, water trickling through the gap between the gates that held back the sea water. Up on to the path, over the crest of a small hill and the beach opened in front of them. Parents out walking with their children, shepherded them up on to the grass as the drunk rabble approached. One of the rabbles laughed and made a rude hand gesture which made one of the mother's cover her young daughter's eyes with her hands. Another chorus of laughter and cursing.

Lukas had managed to make his way onto the sand and was staggering towards the sea. It was calm with mini waves breaking on the shore. It attracted him like a moth going towards a flame. Before he knew what was happening, his feet were soaking and getting wetter by the second as the waves lapped around his feet. He laughed a drunken laugh before sitting down in the water. Another laugh and then two of his friends staggered over, put an arm under each arm pit and hoisted him back to his feet.

"You know what?" He slurred, as he turned to the young bespectacled man on his left.

"No. What?" Came the slurred reply.

"I'm bored."

"I thought you were Lukas. Pleased to me you Bored."

Lukas and the whole group erupted into laughter before he raised one arm, for some reason the other was not working or had gone on strike, to silence them. "Let us go to that little village on the outskirts of town. I hear there is a barmaid there with a nice set...." The rest of the sentence was drowned out by a rousing roar of approval.

5 – A Quiet Drink

Fallon pushed open the door of the Drowned Neighbours and held it open allowing Molly-Beth and pram to enter. For an afternoon, the place was quiet. Joyce was behind the bar, Cyril was sitting in his usual place at the end of the bar and raised his half empty glass in acknowledgement, both Fallons nodded in his direction, and a young brunette was busy clearing tables and wiping them down. Whilst Molly-Beth and pram went to a table, Fallon walked up to the bar.

"Joyce." He greeted.

"Mister Fallon. Your usual?" She said, her hand hovering over the foxglove taps.

"Please and a lemonade for Molly." He opened his wallet and handed over a couple of notes.

"Susie will bring them across when they're ready." She delved into the till and gave him his change.

Fallon stopped, looked over at Cyril and returned to the bar. "Give Cyril a top up too." Joyce smiled and nodded. Cyril raised is glass once more just as another took its place.

"You are a real gent, Mister Fallon. A real gent."

Susie came across and deposited his foxglove ale in a pint glass, while Molly-Beth's lemonade was in a tall thin glass with ice, which chinked against the sides when she lifted it to take a drink. The barmaid returned to her work just as the front door almost came off its hinges and six youngsters staggered in, shouting, and swearing. Students.

"I ask you to mind your language, boys." Cautioned Joyce. The group paused, looked at each other then they burst out laughing. The leader, a tall blonde, blue eyed youth staggered forward and propped himself up against the bar.

"Six pints of your finest, landlord and make it snappy." He tossed a pile of notes on the bar top as if it were wastepaper and joined his friends who were sitting at a table in the corner. The noise they were making now reached annoyance levels. Susie struggled across to them with a tray ladened down by their order. She placed each glass in front of each of the men before turning to leave. The blonde grabbed her wrist. She froze. "Where are you going, my beauty? Why do not you sit on my lap and show me some of that famous local hospitality." He tapped his lap and tried to pull her on to it.

"Please Sir. I am not that kind of girl." Susie pleaded and tried to pull away.

"Not yet, you're not!" He slurred. His friends burst into a chorus of laughter and started to egg him on. Susie broke away and tried to make it to the bar, but the blonde grabbed her waist preventing her. "Come here!" He tried to kiss her as she fought.

Then a voice came from across the room. It was cold and menacing. "Let the girl go."

"What?"

"Let the girl go, drink up and leave."

Blonde put his hand over his eyebrows to shade his eyes allowing him to focus into the gloom. Fallon was on his feet facing him.

"And who's gonna make me?"

"You don't wanna go down that road, kid." Fallon warned, moving slightly closer, spurring blonde's friends to get to their feet and stand behind him.

"And why not?"

"Because that road leads to a world of pain."

"Do you know who I am?"

"Nope. Do not care. A bully is a bully no matter where he is from."

"I am Lukas Falcone. My father could buy this pitiful place and raise it to the ground."

"He could but you are here, and your father isn't. So why do not you be a nice little boy and run-away home before someone gets hurt."

"Jonathan." Molly-Beth grabbed his wrist. She was standing with him. "Please don't." She looked back at the pram.

"Yeah, Jonathan. Listen to the little lady." Lukas mocked.

Fallon tapped the back of her hand gently and eased her back to her chair out of harm's way just as Lukas

36

launched his sneak attack. He tried to punch Fallon in the back. It landed sending Fallon sprawling to the floor. The group laughed and applauded. Fallon picked himself up and turned to face his aggressor.

"Pretty good, kid but that was your freebie."

"How many chances do I get?" Lukas asked looking around at his friends puffing his chest out like a cockerel trying to impress the hens in the yard.

"Two more." Fallon for some unknown reason kept his hands down. Lukas swung again. This time catching Fallon on the jaw, making him stagger a little, but unlike the last time, he did not go down. Instead, he wiped the trickle of blood from the corner of his mouth, nodding as he did so. "That's your special offer." The sound of stool legs scraping backwards across the floor told Fallon, that Cyril was getting to his feet. Fallon raised a hand shaking his head.

"What's the last one?" Asked Lukas, his ego now writing cheques his body was not going to be able to cash.

"You pay for it." Lukas swung but this time Fallon blocked it with his right arm, burying his left fist deep in Lukas' stomach, causing him to tumble backwards into his friends. They were now like angry hornets as they came out swarming, but they stopped. Cyril stood beside his friend as did Molly-Beth, all three poised for action.

"That's enough!" Shouted Joyce as the sound of two hammers clicked into place. The group turned to see her pointing a sawn-off shotgun in their direction.

"But you only have two shots." Lukas pointed out.

"Have you ever seen the mess one of those things can make to a body?" Asked Fallon stepping back. Lukas shook his head. "Then I suggest you leave." Lukas scrambled to his feet shaking off any assistance from members of his group. They bailed out the front door quicker than they came in and as everything calmed down and returned to normal, Joyce brought over fresh drinks and an extra for herself.

"Jesus, Mary and Joseph!" She cursed as she sat down. "That was a bit o' fun was it not?"

"Just a bit."

"Excuse me for asking Mister Fallon but what is it you do?"

"I work for the British Government dealing in special projects."

"A sort of government problem solver?" Joyce suggested taking a gulp from her drink.

"More of a trouble-shooter." Said Fallon giving a sideways glance to his wife as she almost choked on her drink.

Three hours later, a telephone rang. The door from the study opened, and a tall well-built man, well over six feet in height and wearing a white suit, matching shirt, and a pencil thin black tie, exited, and headed towards it as it cried out for attention like a newborn chick opening its mouth for food when one of its parent's returns to the nest. The movement of the man was ballet-like. Each step placed and thought out. His bald head glistened like a cue ball as the light bounced off it. When he spoke, it was precise and measured. The call only lasted a moment before he laid down the receiver on the table, before making his way across the hall to a large wooden door. He knocked on it, waited till he heard a muffled sound from within before entering. He stood in the doorway and coughed politely. The man at the desk looked up.

"It is Master Lukas, Sir. There has been some trouble."

"What trouble? I sent him to that back woods university to keep him out of trouble. Merde!" The man banged his fists on the tabletop before jumping to his feet. He stormed out of the room and grabbed the receiver. "Oui, c'est ton Pèrer. What do you mean someone beat you up in a pub? Did you catch this fool's name? Fallon. Jonathan Fallon. Did you do anything to provoke him? Non. C'est bon. Do nothing." The man hung up the receiver and turned to the man in the white suit. "Monsieur Shalamar, find out everything you can about Monsieur Jonathan Fallon."

"At once, Monsieur Falcone."

On the other end of the line, Lukas hung up and looked around the room at his followers. The fire in his eyes told the group this was not over, and they waited with bated breath.

"What did he say, Lukas?" Asked the buck-toothed spectacled youth.

"We've to do nothing."

"Okay then." snorted the youth.

"Where do you think you are going?" Snapped Lukas that halted the departing throng in their tracks.

"You said..." said a large neanderthal sized man from the doorway of the dorm room.

39

"I know what my father said, imbecile! But he is not me!"

"But if he finds out..." Neanderthal again.

"He won't." He called them over and signalled for the door to be closed. "No one makes a fool of a Falcone and gets away with it. That bastard and his family are going to pay."

6 – Ambush

After the fun and games at the pub, both Fallon and Molly-Beth walked slowly back to the manor house. Cyril had offered to give them a lift in his cart because he did not trust those ruddy students and thought they might return for seconds. He was right. As they came over the hill, Fallon was the first to see them. Four of them blocking the road. He instinctively reached inside his jacket for his CP-2 automatic then remembered it was back at the manor in his safe. He cursed his bad luck as he shepherded Molly-Beth and pram back down the hill.

"What? What's going on, Jonathan?" Asked Molly-Beth startled.

"It'll be fine, Molls. Just keep walking." Their pace quickened.

"Where do you think you're going?" Asked a familiar if unwanted voice. Lukas came from behind a tree on the Fallons left. Several others appeared lining the road on each side. They started to shout and jeer as the Fallons passed them, their pace a run. Then they were brought to a hault as the neanderthal sized student stepped into the road as if someone had chopped down a massive human sized tree to block their way.

"You ain't goin' nowhere Missy." Said neanderthal as he reached out with his massive arms. Molly-Beth lashed out. A kick to the groin area, making the man mountain buckle and squeal in pain. Her action was rewarded by a slap across the face from one of the other students, who was wearing a university sweatshirt with his surname on the back, and the club he belonged to - swimming. It is a university thing. Fallon picked his fallen wife up and together they tried to protect the pram and its tiny occupant.

"You, okay?" Fallon asked. His wife nodded as she raised her fists, as he did. They managed to get in several good blows before both were overwhelmed by the sheer numbers. Fallon hit the ground first under a barrage of kicks and punches, whilst Molly-Beth was incapacitated by the neanderthal, who's vice like grip started to suck the life out of her so much, she passed out.

"Enough." Ordered Lukas. "Don't kill her. I want to have some fun with her first and then we can sell her baby to a friend of my father's." A look of shock fell upon the ensemble. Lukas looked at his gang straight faced for a moment before bursting out into laughter. "I am joking. We'll keep her for a couple of days before releasing her. I got to teach this bastard a lesson." He turned and kicked a downed Fallon in the stomach, like he was trying to score a field goal in rugby. Two of the others laid into Fallon as well, like

4 2

they were trying to gain favour with Lukas by copying him.

Fallon doubled up under the assault and moaned. He tried to look up as the ensemble walked away, one pushing the pram making baby noises whilst neanderthal had Molly-Beth draped over his shoulder like a scarf. "Au Revoir, Monsieur Fallon." Said Lukas in a high-pitched voice, saluting him with the first two fingers of his left hand, like you would a beaten or vanquished foe.

"Monsieur Falcone."

Falcone looked up from his sun lounger next to the pool. His wide brimmed Panama hat shielding his eyes from the sun. It was Shalamar. His huge frame blocked out the sun, or it was scared to peek around. Anyway, Falcone suddenly found himself in shadow.

"Oui."

"It would appear we have a problem."

"How so?"

"You asked me to find out all we knew about Jonathan Fallon."

"Oui. I remember." Falcone removed his sunglasses and placed them down on the table next to him and took a sip from a flute filled with champagne.

"Jonathan Fallon works for the Office of Special Projects. A former army officer."

"Office of Special Projects. That is familiar to me." He got to his feet and untied his bath robe revealing his tan muscular torso and black swimming trunks. Shalamar opened his mouth to speak but Falcone raised an index finger. "Not before my swim." He went up on to the

43

diving board and with one powerful flex of his legs, dove in and swam a full length underwater before surfacing at the other end and climbing out. Shalamar was there with his robe. "Continue."

"The Office of Special Projects is a department of the British Intelligence Service that worked covertly during the last war, and we believe sabotaged 'Project Phoenix'…"

"Project Phoenix?"

"We invested funds in Egypt to try and destabilise the government, by bombing the high-level meeting of the heads of the Bedouin tribes and manufactured the attack in such a way that it would be blamed on the British, several years ago."

"Ah yes, I remember this now. Did our agent Riga return for that?"

"Oui, Monsieur but he was tragically killed in an alley a couple of years later. The police report says he was shot in the back." (*What Falcone and the authorities did not know, was that Riga was killed at Ashton Manor by Fallon and Forrester dealt with the 'situation'*).

"A pity. I had such plans for him in our Berlin office." He walked over and took another sip from his glass before resuming his position on the lounger. "But such is the price of business. Were his family compensated?"

"According to our sources, the German police arrested them a few days later, thanks to a tip off, and they found two million marks in his bank account. They managed to trace the money back to a heist in Dusseldorf a few months previously."

4 4

"Very good, Monsieur Shalamar. Very good indeed." He put his sunglasses back on and settled down to read his book, finishing by saying, "now all we need now, is for that idiot son of mine, not to do anything stupid."

When Fallon finally opened his eyes, he found himself looking up at the white painted ceiling of his master bedroom. He sighed with relief. It had all been a dream. Then he tried to move, the wave of pain that shot through his body told him that it had been real. He slowly lifted the sheets and looked down at his battered and bruised body. He gingerly tried to sit up. Pain. He swung his legs over the side of the bed. Pain. He swore. His feet contacted the carpet. Pain. Swore. He pushed himself away from the bed and screamed with pain. The door flew open, and Smithers rushed in just in time to catch him.

"What the hell are you doing?" He scolded.

"Gotta gets up. Gotta find Molly and Peter."

"All in good time. The police have been notified and are looking into it."

"The police!" Laughed Fallon then grabbed his sides as they were racked with pain. "They couldn't find their own arses even if you gave them a map!" He tried to get up again but was pushed back down by Smithers.

"The doc says you've to lie there for at least a fortnight."

"Two weeks. What about..." Fallon protested.

"Two weeks. Do I have to get Cyril and the boys to come and help me tie you to the bed?" Fallon shook his head and lay back. "Anyway, the police thing was

4 5

procedure. I have also informed the Colonel and he has put the full resources of the OSP at our disposal."

"Thank him for me, will you?"

"Already done. I've also taken the liberty of asking the boys to use their contacts and see if we can get the whereabouts of Ms Molly and the young master." The '*boys*' he was referring to were of course, Jenkins and Baldwin, both of whom had extensive underworld connections before the war and swore blind to the Judge sentencing them, that that part of their lives was over. So, the magistrate gave them a choice – prison or military service. They chose the latter and that is how they met Smithers at the OSP and ended up working for Fallon at the Manor.

The next day, an expensive looking car pulled up in front of the manor, a man in a chauffeur's outfit, grey jacket, trousers, and peaked cap got out of the driver's side and made his way around to the other side of the car, opening the rear door, allowing his passenger to climb out. The overweight gentleman was wearing a dark suit, waist coat, white shirt, and a red tie with a Windsor knot. A white carnation popped its head out of the buttonhole on the left-hand side. He straightened himself up just as his chauffeur handed him several paper files, which he tucked under his arm. He took a deep breath. The way someone would if they were coming to give you some sad news.

The doorbell rang and Smithers went downstairs to answer. He turned the brass door handle and opened the door, and seeing who was in front of him, immediately stood at attention. No salute. Just poker straight.

"Aren't you going to invite me in, Captain?" Asked the visitor.

"Sorry Sir. Please come in." Smithers moved to the side allowing the visitor to enter. "To what do we owe this pleasure, Sir?"

"This Fallon business. Very nasty. How is K-Twelve?"

"Battered and bruised, Sir but I'll survive." Came the response from the top of the stairs. Fallon gingerly walked down the stairs, step by painful step, using the banister for support.

"Dreadful business." Repeated the arrival, as he made his way to the living room and sat down on the couch. He laid the folders he had been carrying down beside him. "Any news on K-9 and the infant?"

"Molly and Peter, Sir." Corrected Fallon easing himself into one of the vacant chairs.

"Yes. Yes. Of course. Please forgive me."

"Our contacts believe they are being held in a vacant student accommodation just outside town." Said Smithers. "The Greyfield Estate." Fallon looked across at him with a *'when were you going to tell me'* look on his face. Smithers just shrugged his shoulders. "We believe they are being held in the grounds-keeper's cottage just back from the main gate, by at least eight to ten individuals. One of these is Lukas Falcone." A look of recognition appeared on the arrival's face.

He reached over and picked up the top file and handed it to Smithers, who opened it and after digesting the contents read aloud. "Lukas Falcone. A French national. Age twenty. Son of French Industrialist Alexandre

47

Falcone. Lukas is studying politics at the local university and is in his third year. Has had several scrapes with the law but not been charged. A couple of counts of rape and one of actual bodily harm. Acquitted of all."

"His father has some influence, then." Commented Fallon shifting his weight in the chair as he tried to gain a more comfortable position.

"That, dear boy, is an understatement." Commented the arrival who picked up the next file and opened it himself, reading: "Alexandre Falcone. French national. Age approximately fifty-five. Head of Falcone Industries in Paris but has offices globally. Made his first fortune in oil before branching out into diamonds, gold, and property. Linked to several revolutions in the underdeveloped world and several disappearances of competitors. Nothing ever proven."

"As slippery as his son..." Commented a disgusted Fallon.

"OSP thinks he is the mastermind behind your little jaunt in Egypt five years ago, but we have little or no proof. Every time we get close, the lead either vanishes or ends up dead. As far as the people in power are concerned, Falcone is as clean as the white pressed suits he wears." He tossed over another file which contained a photograph and a brief dossier. "He is never seen in public without the man in the picture. Goes by the name of Shalamar.

His head of security and chief bodyguard. A nasty piece of work. Started as a strongman in the circus before using his talents as an assassin for hire. Not sure how he came into Falcone's orbit of influence, but he just suddenly appeared at his side and has been there ever since. Likes to use his brute strength to dispatch opponents up close or sometimes uses a knife. Always immaculately dressed and is rumoured to speak several languages."

"Where does Falcone stay?" Asked Fallon standing up and walking to the window.

"He owns a private Island off the coast. Kalander Island, it is called." The arrival closed the folder and placed it on the table. "Falcone senior should not be your concern now. The life of your wife and child should be."

"Colonel. It has believe me. Didn't you teach us during training, that it is family?"

"Ah yes. '*Familia Super Omnia*' as my Latin professor used to say." Colonel Forrester was famous in the security service circles for his use of Latin phrases during his pep-talks. No one was ever sure whether this fabled Latin professor existed, but no one ever dared to question Forrester. "Anyway, another couple of days rest and recuperation and we'll see what we can do to sort out this little business, huh?" Forrester got to his feet and made his way to the door. "Two days' rest. Ante stercore percusserit fan." He chuckled to himself as he opened the door, gave them a brief wave and he was gone.

"Ante stercore percusserit fan?" Asked Fallon.

"Before the shit hits the fan." Translated Smithers shaking his head, as he put his arm around Fallon's waist and helped him back up the stairs.

49

7 – Information Received

The extra few days that Fallon took to recover, allowed his friends time to do some preparation work, as he found out, when he was summoned into the study. In the room, gathered around the table were Smithers, Baldwin, Cyril, Jenkins and even 'Sparks,' who sat nervously off to the side with a large suitcase beside him. As he entered the room, the scene reminded Fallon of his days, long since gone, in the military, minutes before the start of a mission, where everyone involved would come together and contribute to a brainstorming session. Planning every detail down to the smallest point. Making every contingency plan in case something was to go wrong. The conversation stopped, just as he walked in making him feel on edge.

"Jesus! Has someone just died!" He exclaimed trying his best to lighten the mood.

"We've just been reviewing Baldwin's Intel." Said Smithers pointing to a piece of paper on the table. The paper turned out to be a very roughly draw map.

If Fallon had not known the author, he would have sworn an infant in kindergarten had drawn it. The map showed the layout of the entrance to the Greyfield Estate. A hastily drawn straight line at the bottom had an arrow pointing to it saying, 'main road,' there was another set of parallel lines heading up the page, which Fallon assumed was the road going into the estate.

Low and behold, there was another arrow and heading 'road to main house' further up the page. There were squiggly lines on both sides of the 'road to main house' and the word 'trees' written in. On the left-hand side, after the trees was a crude rectangle with 'barn' scrawled in the middle. Whilst on the right-hand side, tucked in behind the trees, was the grounds-keeper's cottage where they thought Molly and the baby were being held.

"I fink there's maybe three snobs in the barn," said Baldwin using a pencil as a pointer, "a further four walking the grounds wif abou' three in the cottage."

"That's ten." Counted Fallon. "Any of these Falcone."

"I fink he's in the cottage, Sir." Replied Baldwin.

"Thank you." Fallon leaned over and surveyed the map. "In through the main gate?" He suggested.

"Frontal assault might alert them and put Molly and young Peter into harm's way." Said Smithers. "Why not use a multi-sided attack." Over the next half hour, the group bounced ideas backwards and forwards. Each suggestion was vetted on its pros and cons. Most were rubbished until they all agreed on one. Then 'Sparks' jumped into life like someone turned him on at the wall.

"And I have just the tools to help us." He lifted the large suitcase on to the table, clicked both locks open, and through back the lid, revealing a treasure trove of automatic pistols and several large machine guns.

He took out one of the automatics. "Gentlemen. This is the Colt Model 1911A1. Since our American friends joined us in the last war, they have made great innovations into the production of firearms. It uses a seven round magazine and uses a point four five calibre round. Recoil or single action. The Yanks call it the Colt 45." He passed them out. Each man weighing it. Feeling it.

Pulling back the slider. Checking the magazine. "Also, from our friends across the pond, allow me to introduce you to a prototype machine gun - the Thompson M1928A1 – or 'Tommy Gun'. These are straight off the production line thanks to the Colonel and his contacts in the American Government. It uses the same ammunition as the automatic pistol, in a twenty round box style magazine." He handed one out to those who wished a look. Jenkins let out a whistle of amazement as he looked the machine gun over.

"The Yanks refer to it as the Chicago Typewriter." Added Jenkins. The others looked at him surprised that he would know such a piece of information like that. Jenkins looked back with a playful look on his face and shrugged his shoulders.

"We could've used a couple of these on that Soho job back in Nineteen, eh Baldie?" Baldwin nodded in agreement, like a child would if he were in a candy store, and you asked him to pick anything he wanted.

5 2

"What about the CP-2?" Asked Fallon looking for his service weapon.

"I'm afraid the Cuthbertson Prototype version two has been retired, Sir. The Colonel's orders. Each operative has been assigned the forty-five." Replied 'Sparks' looking a little dejected.

Gerald 'Sparks' Cuthbertson was the armourer, and supply officer for the Office of Special Projects. It was standard operating procedure, and very wise, to visit him before you left on an assignment. You never really knew what to expect when you entered his little 'toyshop,' as he referred to his department. It had started in Egypt as a little warehouse somewhere on base and referred to as AB-25, but since the OSP had been absorbed into the Intelligence Service after the war, he had been given a floor in the main building, all be it the basement level, and people, scientists, and people with imagination, to work under him. Fallon often expected to meet the Mad Hatter from 'Alice in Wonderland' down there, but to this date, never has.

"All I want is Molly and Peter returned home safely." They all nodded in agreement. "And I want Falcone and that huge bastard who put his hands on my wife." He pulled back the slider on the Colt and released it to underline his point. "No one else must get harmed. Understood?" They nodded. "They are just sheep, but Falcone is the Wolf." He straightened his arm and pulled the trigger as if he were trying to shoot an imaginary target. Click!

"I have something that might help you with that, K-Twelve." Announced 'Sparks' rummaging around in the bottom of the case. "Ah, here they are." And he brought out what looked like marbles, the kind you tossed about in the playground when you were a child. "On your Egyptian assignment, remember I gave you toothpaste that was actually an explosive." Fallon and Smithers remembered. "Well, these little beauties I have called 'nite-nite' bombs. You see, you roll them along the ground towards your target and if you are lucky enough, one of them will stand on one, they crush the cylinder, and it releases a powerful knock-out gas, effective within five feet. Crunch, and they'll be out for at least an hour."

"Sneaky little chap, aren't you?" Remarked Cyril picking up a couple of marbles to inspect them before 'Sparks' intervened and put them into a small velvet bag before handing it to Smithers, who carefully put the bag in his pocket.

Several hours before this meeting, the telephone rang in Falcone's mansion. Shalamar answered it and after a few minutes of conversation, his face paled. "One moment." He placed the receiver down on the table and went into the study. "It is Lukas for you Monsieur."

"What is it, Shalamar?" Falcone asked puzzled by the look on his chief of security's face.

"I think you should take this call, Monsieur."

"Hallo." Said Falcone picking up the receiver.

"It is me, Papa." Announced Lukas.

"Oui."

"I have done it."

"Done what, Boy?"

"Something that will make you proud of me."

"Spit it out."

"I have taken care of that bastard Fallon and I have his wife and child as a prize." He crowed.

"YOU HAVE DONE WHAT?" Falcone screamed into the mouthpiece. The veins on the side of his neck bulging. "I told you not to do anything!"

"But Papa. I am a Falcone, and that piece of shit Fallon, embarrassed me in front of my friends."

"Your friends? That rabble you hang about with aren't even in the same social class as you, you imbecile!"

"But you have always told me that if someone does you wrong, a show of vulnerability is a sign of weakness and weakness is not in the Falcone code." Lukas protested.

"Do you know who this piece of sheet as you call him actually is?"

"Non. And do I care?"

"He works for the British Government as a spy. He kills people for a living and what did you just do? Kidnap the one thing that is more precious to a man than life itself – his family."

"I can handle him, Papa."

"My God. For once, use what little brains you have. He will be coming for them and for YOU."

"But Papa...."

"No buts. I will plan for the woman and the child to come to the Island. I want you to come with them."

"But I'm not afraid."

"You should be." Falcone hissed menacingly before hanging up and looking over at Shalamar. "Get my yacht

55

ready to sail to the mainland and pick up that cargo. Make sure that that idiot of a son of mine comes as well."

"And what if he refuses."

"He comes with you."

"Oui Monsieur."

At the main gate, which guarded the exclusive estate that was Greyfield, two guards were aroused from their game of poker by the sound of a dilapidated tractor coming along the road. One of them grabbed his rifle, slinging it over his shoulder, before venturing out to the gate. There at the gate, sitting proudly on a battered old tractor sat Cyril. "Evening Sir." He spoke. "Gotta a trailer load of spuds for the main house."

"This is private property. Go away." Dismissed the guard.

"These spuds were picked fresh this mornin' and are liable to go off unless we get them under cover sharpish."

"What is this word 'spuds' you keep saying, you are annoying little man?" Asked the guard moving closer to the gate and unslinging his weapon as he did so.

"Spuds. PO-TAY-TOES." Replied Cyril saying each syllable of the word slowly with a mixture of micky taking and pity for the ignorance of the man. The guard unlocked the gate allowing the chain to drop to the floor. The gate creaked and clanked open as he approached the tractor.

"Stay where you are and do not move!" Ordered the guard.

"No fear, mate." Said Cyril raising his hands to shoulder height.

The guard checked out one side of the pile of vegetables and even tried to jump up to see the other side. Failing to accomplish this, he moved to the back of the trailer where he was met by Baldwin who dispatched him with a karate chop to the side of the neck. Smithers and Jenkins came around the corner and helped Baldwin deal with the guard.

"I think there's another one in the shack." Whispered Cyril climbing down from the tractor. Smithers nodded and stealthily moved towards the shack. He managed to get to the side of the building before a voice called out from inside.

"Klaus, where are you? This hand is getting cold as is my ass. Come in and close the door." Smithers edged forward but had to crouch as he went under the window. The others, meanwhile, waited patiently back at the trailer. He got to the door and pulled out a couple of 'marbles' that 'Sparks' had given him and rolled them on to the floor of the shack and waited. "Klaus, I swear to God I am going to kick your German...." CRUNCH! Then nothing. Smithers popped his head around the corner quickly before darting back to behind the safety of the wall. Waited a few seconds for a response, not receiving one, looked again. The guard was face down on the floor, out for the count. Smithers stood up.

"As 'Sparks' would say – nite nite."

At the back of the trees on the left-hand side, Fallon had made his way round to the back of the barn. Through a crack in the wood, he looked in and saw five individuals huddled around a campfire eating food, smoking, and drinking. He delved into the pockets of his coat and pulled out several more 'marbles' before slinking his way around to the front door. He noticed that the light from the campfire had illuminated a gap between the floor and the main door, large enough for him to toss in the marbles, which he promptly did but they rolled well short of the group getting caught up in the mixture of straw and dirt that was on the floor. He cursed his luck.

Then remembering what 'Sparks' had said about the range of his toys, he quietly knocked on the door. RATATATAT. Nothing. RATATATAT. Slightly louder this time. Someone stirred. He recognised him. It was the buck-toothed kid from the group that attacked him. 'Toothy' got to his feet and moved towards the door but stopped inches from the marbles. Fallon softly punched the framework in frustration and cursed.

RATATATAT. He did it even louder and to his delight, 'Toothy' heard it as he moved closer. CRUNCH! CRUNCH! Went the marbles and within seconds, the occupants of the barn joined the guards in la-la-land.

"Sparks should use these at the Office Christmas Party. It would be a knockout." Said Fallon as he went to join the others who had assembled outside the grounds-keeper's cottage. Smoke moved aimlessly from the chimney and the light from the large window above lit up the crouching group's faces. They quickly and silently slipped back into the safety of the shadows. Smithers gave out a hissing whistle that attracted Fallon's attention and he joined them at the rear of the cottage.

"The guards are out." Reported Baldwin.

"The group in the barn won't be joining us either." Informed Fallon pulling out his automatic and slowly pulling back the slide and releasing it. "Remember, I want the thug that hurt Molly and Lukas. Any others, we leave for the authorities." He looked around to check everyone was clear. They were. Smithers and Baldwin cocked their machine guns. Jenkins stayed back at the tractor with Cyril, both acting as lookouts. Jenkins armed with a machine gun whilst Cyril had brought along his trusted twelve bore. Did not trust the foreign muck was his response when they offered him his choice of the Colt or the Thompson.

Smithers and Baldwin took up position either side of the door with weapons at the ready. Fallon put his hand on the door handle and turned it slowly. He mouthed 1-2-3 before yanking it open and the three men spilled into the building. Neanderthal was caught with his pants down urinating into a bucket, while a young half naked blonde female screamed as she tried to pull up the bed clothes to cover her modesty. Neanderthal did not know whether to raise his hands, or cover his groin, the strain evident on his face as he tried to make several decisions at once. They searched the cottage but no sign of Molly or Peter.

Lukas was nowhere to be seen either. "Get the girl outa here." Ordered Fallon. Baldwin tossed the girl his jacket before ushering her outside. "Get your pants back on." Fallon hissed levelling the barrel of the Colt at Neanderthal's forehead. The hammer cocked, his finger tightening on the trigger. "Where are they?"

59

"Who?"

"My wife and child."

"Lukas took them. Yes, he did. He took them." Neanderthal gave a throaty laugh. Fallon's trigger finger shook as he struggled to control himself.

"Where...did...he...take...them?" He said each word slowly and precisely.

"His Papa's got an Island. Yes, he does. His Papa's got an Island."

"Where is it?"

Neanderthal fell silent and look straight into Fallon's tortured eyes. "Not gonna tell you. Nope. Not gonna tell you. Tis a secret."

"TELL ME!" Fallon screamed pressing the barrel of the gun so hard against the boy's forehead that it made an imprint on it when he pulled back.

"Nope." Repeated the youngster looking around with a pleased as punch smile on his face. This riled Fallon who slammed his fists down on the table making everyone jump.

"Jonathan." Called a calming voice behind Fallon. It was Smithers. Fallon spun around. Tears streaming down his face. "Let Jenkins find out where the Island is. He has a knack for this kind of stuff." As if on cue, Jenkins appeared behind Smithers and edged his way to the front. He was carrying a brown handyman's tool bag.

"Don't worry Sir, I'll soon have this young man singing like a canary. Just you wait and see." Jenkins placed his tool bag on the bed and opened it revealing various 'tools' of the trade. Hammers. Saws. Chisels.

Spanners and pliers. "Mister Smithers, be a mate, and bring over that small table will ya?" Smithers did as he was asked and placed the table in front of the now seated and bound Neanderthal. The stupid smile that once split his face in half had long since disappeared. "His right hand, if you please."

Despite trying to resist, the thug's right hand was placed and secured by Smithers on the table. Jenkins looked at the hand, then at his array of tools, then back at the hand before picking up a ball pin hammer. He tapped the rounded bit softly a couple of times before bringing it down hard just next to the now terrified thug. "Can you splay his fingers out please?" Smithers, after some effort, managed. The Neanderthal struggled again his terrified saucer like eyes darting between Fallon, Smithers, and Jenkins. Fallon just stood there allowing his rage to fuel his desire to watch what was about to happen. "Now, my boss asked you where they have taken his lovely lady wife and their son. Are you gonna tell me or do I have to get nasty?"

Neanderthal shook his head defiantly. He screamed as his little finger disintegrated as it met the downward force of the hammer. He whimpered and once again looked to Fallon as his savour. "Where are they?" Again, a shake of the head. Again, another blood curdling scream as another finger was crushed between wood and metal. "You have eight more chances before we turn to your toes, then your groin...do you really want to put yourself through all that pain and hurt. Just tell us, where did they take them?"

"K...K.... Kal.... Kalander Island." Neanderthal blurted out. Smithers released his hands which he instinctively grabbed and cradled like a new-born. He looked up at Fallon, tears streaming down his face. "Why did you do this to me?" He asked. "Why?"

Fallon walked across and looked down at the pitiful wretch in front of him. "Because for me, it's family above all." He almost spat the words out. Neanderthal whimpered cradling his damaged hand.

"What do you want us to do with him, boss?" Asked Jenkins as he picked up his bag.

"Leave him for the police." This brought a faint glimmer of a smile to the thug's face which made Fallon bend over him almost getting nose to nose with him as he warned. "When the police arrive, you tell them why someone did this to you. If you mention any names, we will be back, and I will kill you! Do you understand?" Neanderthal nodded.

Fallon and the rest of them departed, heading back to the Estate. Still high on the thrill of the night's events, Fallon picked up the telephone and phoned Forrester. To begin with, his superior was far from amused at what they had done but after Fallon told him the intel they had received, the older man relented and said he was willing to help. After a five-minute conversation, Fallon came into the lounge where the others were sitting expectantly. He painfully walked over to the drinks table and poured himself a drink, milking the suspense like the director Alfred Hitchcock would become famous for in the movies he would make decades later.

"Well?" Asked Smithers.

"The Colonel will supply us with all the Intel we need about the island. The planning and carrying out of the mission are down to us." Fallon went over to the desk in the corner and took out several pieces of paper from one of the drawers, placing them down on the table in front of the men. "We now must produce a plan to rescue Molly and Peter. Any ideas?"

"Excuse me, Sir…" Jenkins raised his hand, "…what about something along the lines of the Trojan horse." The group were stunned. Not just because they had not credited Jenkins to be so well read, but the basis of the idea just might work, but it would need some flushing out. The discussion carried on well into the next day. A mountain of paper on the floor was evidence of the discarded ideas. Once everyone agreed with the principal of the plan, Fallon was back on the telephone to Forrester bringing him up to speed, requesting an essential part of the plan from him. Without hesitation, Forrester agreed.

8 – Kalander Island

Kalander Island sits some five hundred miles off the coast of the mainland, gently caressed by the North Atlantic Ocean. From the air, it looks like a giant fried egg with the yoke, Le lac des âmes or Lake of Souls, down at the bottom end. It is eighty-five kilometres long and about forty five kilometres wide with three main towns – Santa Helena, which serves at the main port and dropping off point for tourists: Santa Sophia, in the South of the Island and Santa Paulina, the capital and administrative head of the Island. It is owned by Falcone Industries, who purchased it off the French, at a knock down price, the discount given as a thank you to them for aiding the French in their fight against the Germans in the Great War that finished only a couple of years previous.

Its main source of revenue is the large Falcone Industries complex to the north of the Island which employs most of the Populus, some one hundred thousand souls who live in and around the three towns.

There are various off-shoots of Falcone Industries through-out the Island, all supplying the main complex with raw materials.

Lukas and two of his minions had hopped a ride on Falcone's yacht, along with their prize – Molly-Beth and young Peter. The trip lasted an age but eventually, the boat tied up at Falcone's private berth and unloaded its cargo. Falcone had sent three cars to pick up his guests. As per usual, Lukas and his friends had made use of the onboard refreshments and were worse for wear. In fact, Lukas would have fallen sideways off the gang plank into the water, if it had not been for the lightning reactions of Shalamar who grabbed his arm in a vice like grip, making him squeal with pain. Shalamar just looked down at him with a glare.

Lukas' companions both staggered over to the car, a Pierce-Arrow 7-passenger touring car, and got in the back then proceeded to vomit on the floor. Shalamar rolled his eyes as the three juveniles roared with laughter as if this were the funniest thing they had ever seen.

Shalamar motioned a second car, a McFarlane twin Valve Six Touring 147, forward and held out his hand. Molly-Beth took it. "My apologies for them, Madame. They are immature little pricks!" Said Shalamar as he helped her into the back of the second car, being careful to mind young Peter who was cradled in her other arm. He gently closed the door and signalled for the driver to leave. The 'vomit' car pulled in behind, with Lukas standing on the foot plate that ran along both sides of the car. Shalamar was in the car in front.

Lukas yelled and screamed egging his driver to go faster. He refused.

After a few minutes of tomfoolery, Lukas calmed down slightly and then started to imitate a bird in flight, flapping one arm frantically whilst holding on to the door mirror with the other. Another Pierce-Arrow made up the trio that departed the dock. Falcone had a passion for American made automobiles, having several in his collection that he kept in a huge garage on his estate.

Falcone estate is situated high up on a hill where Alexandre Falcone can look down on the world, like some all-powerful God. Security is tight. The walls that surround the estate are high and topped with barbed wire. Armed guards patrol during the day whilst guards with dogs patrol during the night. Entry is through a guarded main gate, invite only.

The cavalcade powered its way into the compound where Falcone was standing at the top of the steps that led to the main house. At first, he was pleased to see his son return but that mood soon changed when he saw the state of him. His car had not even stopped when Lukas tried to put a foot on the ground. The continued momentum of the car caused him to lose his grip on the mirror and break into a drunken, swaying run in a vain attempt to both save face and stop himself from falling on his face. The run failed and he ate dirt. He lay there for a moment before rolling over and kicking his legs up in the air like a toddler having a tantrum as he laughed an alcohol fuelled laugh. His companions fell out the back of the car, took one look at him, pointed, and then joined in in the jollity. Falcone's face changed to one of fury. His hands on his hips.

"What the bloody hell do you think you are doing?" He yelled.

"Who's the old man, Lukas? Your butler?" Joked one of his companions.

As soon as his father spoke, Lukas miraculously sobered up getting slowly to his feet and dusting himself down, his head hanging in shame as his father stared down at him. The identity of Lukas' father was lost on his companions as they grabbed each other and started to dance around the courtyard. One even tried to climb into the ornate fountain in the middle and pretended to bathe. Lukas walked slowly up the stairs but stopped one below his father, head still bowed.

"We will talk about this later!" Snapped Falcone grabbing his son by the scruff of his neck and hauling him inside leaving his two companions frolicking about oblivious. "Monsieur Shalamar, take out the trash!" Came the order from inside before the heavy front door closed. Shalamar smiled as he approached Lukas' companions who looked up at him from their impromptu bath. Shalamar took them separately, one in each hand, around the neck and plunged them simultaneously into the water. Both thrashed about wildly as they both tried to break free and get up to the surface to breathe.

Both stopped moving as Shalamar tightened his grip even more, his fingers gouging into their necks like a sculpturer playing with clay. Blood started to float up from the wounds. One further violent movement and

Shalamar's hands came out of the water dripping wet and holding the two windpipes that he had pulled from the now deceased men. It was days like this, he enjoyed his job. He ordered some of the astonished guards that stood around in shock to dispose of the bodies.

It was then Shalamar realised that Molly-Beth had just witnessed what had transpired. He washed off his hands in the fountain and walked slowly across. She turned her shoulder towards him using it as a shield to protect Peter, tears in her eyes.

"Did you have to do that?" She asked.

"Monsieur Falcone ordered it Madame. It is not wise to go against his wishes." He extended an arm towards the main house. "Your quarters are waiting, Madame. Please." Molly-Beth looked at him once more before turning and heading up the stairs. The main door opened and a Spanish looking woman in her late forties stood there with a welcoming smile on her face. She opened her arms and tried to take Peter, but Molly broke free.

"He's my child and I will look after him." Molly said. The woman took a step back and motioned for her to go into the house.

Falcone appeared back outside. "Bonjour, Madam Fallon. Welcome to my humble abode." Molly just stood there cradling Peter. "I am sorry we had to meet under such unpleasant circumstances. However, you are here now. Whilst you are here, you will be treated with the utmost respect and are free to wander the grounds at your leisure."

"Can I leave the grounds?"

"Sadly, no. Not until this sad business has been resolved. I have set aside a couple of rooms at the top of the house for you and your infant. If you require anything, Maria will attend to you. Please, go with her." Falcone waited until Molly had gone inside before turning to Shalamar, a worried look on his face. "Any news of Fallon?"

"Our sources have heard that he is out looking for his family."

"Merde. I was hoping to deal with this quietly. Do you think he will come here?"

"What would you do in his shoes, Monsieur?"

"I see your point. Do we know of anyone who can deal with this?"

"Someone has just popped up in my research. An unknown but with a very good reputation."

"Unknown?"

"Oui Monsieur. His reputation seemed to appear as if by magic."

"Suspicious."

"Oui. At first, but I have gone through all the regular channels, and he is legit."

"What is this ghost's name?"

"Louis Serpens."

"Ah bon! Make all the necessary introductions. I want him here on the Island as soon as possible."

"Oui, Monsieur. At once." Shalamar went to leave but paused at the door. "Monsieur?"

"Oui?"

"What about Monsieur Lukas?"

69

"Leave him to me."

A week past and Molly started to find her way around the estate, all the while noting the weak and blind spots within the routine of the guards. She would play along with this charade until her husband would come to rescue her. Yes, play along but taking notes. She was allowed free reign of the main house and a couple of the smaller outbuildings but there was a limit. She went for a swim in the large swimming pool at the rear of the house whilst Peter was napping one day. Did a few laps front crawl before climbing out on the far side of the pool. She reached for one of the numerous towels that littered the place and wrapped it around her waist, took a quick glance around.

The guards were pre-occupied with some of the new female staff that had just arrived, so she took her chance to test the security. She moved quickly towards what looked like a guest house and tried the door. It was locked. She cursed her luck before looking over her shoulder as she sensed a presence. The huge hulking mass that went by the name of Shalamar towered above her with his arms folded. He had a huge smile on his face. She smiled back.

"If you please, Madame." He motioned towards the house. Molly sighed and complied.

"Well, you can't blame a girl for trying, Monsieur." And with that, she bounded back towards the main building flanked by a couple of armed guards.

"I would think nothing less of you, Madame. Bon." Whispered Shalamar with a slight hint of admiration in his voice.

9 – Louis Serpens

The ferry, Goddess of the Sea, was an old single stack rust bucket on her last legs. This relic was the only contact the Island had to the mainland. The ferry crossed once a month bringing both goods and tourists to and from the Island. The engine coughed and spluttered like an old maid as it struggled against the swells and currents of the ocean as it made its way into Santa Helena. Santa Helena was billed as the gateway to the Island on all the pamphlets. A picture postcard type of place with beautifully painted harbour front houses that looked like they had been picked out of some oil painting painted by one of the masters.

Fishing boats bobbed up and down at anchor. Seagulls screeched, dive bombing both into the sea and at some of the people on the harbour wall who waved at the ferry as it came in. It took a couple of goes to finally bring the old lady next to the jetty, secure her to the side with rope the thickness of a man's upper leg and then the gang plank was dragged on board and tied into place. A gaggle of tourists, complete with the latest cameras and money to spend in the various souvenir shops that lined the streets, funnelled off the ferry and dispersed.

Last to disembark, was a man dressed all in black wearing dark sunglasses and carrying a small battered brown suitcase. He stopped at the bottom of the plank and slowly looked around before moving off towards the centre of town. The smell of the sea toyed with his nostrils. A mixture of dampness, the sand, and seaweed with a hint of rotting fish that had been left by the fishermen in their creels. It made the man wonder whether one of the major fashion houses had thought of bottling it and turning it into an expensive perfume. *Eau de Mere* would be a good name, he thought, allowing, for a moment, his mind to wander.

Suddenly, there was a wailing noise and a couple of motor bikes with sirens on the handlebars came tearing around the corner making the man stop in his tracks and take avoiding action by jumping on to the pavement. Seconds later, a battered old car came round the corner with a man in uniform sitting importantly in the back. The car stopped next to the man.

"Your papers." Demanded the man in the back of a Fiat 510, a four-door open body model and substantial canvas folding top and side screens, which shielded the occupants from the weather whether it was kind, like it was on this occasion, or harsh which is more common, holding out his hand.

"Who's asking?" Replied the arrival.

"I am Captain Emile Gordona, Chef de la Police." Introduced Gordona as if the arrival would know who he was. The arrival delved into the inside of his jacket and pulled out a French passport and placed it in Gordona's hand. Gordona opened it. "Monsieur Louis Serpens?" The arrival nodded. "Please remove your glasses. I like to see a man's eyes. They are the window to a man's soul you know." The arrival did as he was asked revealing a pair of icy blue eyes. Gordona seemed to go pale under the arrival's gaze and quickly handed back the document. "Are you here for business or pleasure?"

"A bit of both."

"Search him!" Ordered Gordona as one of his men stepped forward. Serpens tensed. "Monsieur, we either do this here or down at the jail? Your choice." Serpens raised his hands in surrender allowing the pat-down. Along the arms, down the sides and then down the middle of the back. The guard got to the waist and stopped. He patted again to confirm before lifting the back of the jacket revealing the butt of a large automatic. Gordona sat bolt upright. "Why do you have this, Monsieur? Are you expecting trouble?" The guard handed the weapon over.

"It pays to be prepared in my job." replied to Serpens.

"And what is your job, Monsieur?"

"I help people with their problems."

"A problem fixer?"

"More of a problem eradicator."

"Arrest him!"

"What for? I've done nothing wrong!" Protested Serpens.

73

"Concealment of a dangerous weapon for starters." The guard reached into his belt and unclipped a set of cuffs.

"That won't be necessary." Said a voice from across the road. Gordona strained his neck round to see who was talking. Again, his colour drained from his face.

"Monsieur Shalamar. Do you know this man?"

"Oui. Monsieur Falcone has invited him to the Island to discuss some business. Is there a problem, Monsieur Chef de la Police ?"

"Non, Monsieur." The police chief motioned with his hand for the guard to put away the cuffs as if he were swatting a fly.

"Then I suggest you go back to what Monsieur Falcone pays you for and stop annoying his guests."

"Oui Monsieur. But of course, Monsieur Shalamar." And with that, the car spluttered into life, the motorbikes blared and off they went up the street.

"My apologises, my friend." Said Shalamar handing Serpens back the automatic.

"Not a problem. In my business, I'm used to it." Serpens put the weapon back into its holster and pulled the jacket back over. As they walked, Shalamar noticed Serpens was wearing a metal bracelet on his left wrist.

"Assassins wear jewellery these days?"

"Oh, this old thing." Dismissed Serpens holding his wrist up so that Shalamar could inspect the bracelet more closely. "A gift from a friend."

"Non Est Optio Defectum. Italian?" Shalamar read the inscription engraved on it.

"Latin. It says failure is not an option. A code, I live by."

The walk was pleasant. The two men chat about this and that, but it was a guarded conversation. Each man giving the other just enough information whilst fishing for titbits from the other.

"I like the look of your weapon."

"Pardon me?" Serpens said slightly taken a back.

"The automatic you have tucked away in the middle of your lower back. Isn't it that new America model?"

"Yip. The Colt '45 Model 1911."

"May I have a look? Guns are my hobby."

"Sure." Serpens took out the Colt and handed it to Shalamar, butt first.

Shalamar inspected the chrome plated weapon, pulling back the slide several times whilst holding it up to his ear to hear how smooth the action was. He released the clip. A copper headed slug peaked out from the top. "Eight rounds?"

"Seven. Point four five ACP." Corrected Serpens.

"Ah." Nodded Shalamar appreciating the weapon. He reminded Serpens of a small boy opening his presents at Christmas and finding that one gift he had always wanted. "Does it have good stopping power?"

"I've had no complaints so far."

Serpens suddenly froze as a cruel expression came over Shalamar's face. He was now pointing the weapon at Serpens, the business end facing him, and he suddenly felt very uncomfortable. Serpens took a couple of steps back raising his hands slowly. However, the cruel expression vanished as quickly as it had appeared.

"My apologises, my friend. I play a little joke on you." Joked Shalamar handing Serpens back his weapon which he put back in the small of his back before anymore little 'jokes' took Shalamar's fancy.

"Wasn't so little." Said Serpens exhaling.

As they continued their stroll up towards Falcone's complex, Shalamar took the time, whilst they chatted, to study his walking companion. Serpens was approximately five foot ten inches in height. In his mid-thirties, he would guess. With bleached blonde hair swept back and kept in place by hair crème or something of the like. A small blonde goatee beard kept his chin warm. The most striking thing about him was his piercing blue eyes that seem to cut into you like ice shards.

Serpens spoke with an accent, obviously, but Shalamar struggled to place it and he was good with accents. This troubled him. He also noticed that Serpens walked uneasily with a slight limp. Strange for a man with such a reputation to have a disability like that. Another thing on the growing list of inconsistencies about Serpens. Shalamar made a mental note to dig deeper into the background of his current companion.

Falcone's complex seemed to rise out of the ground, like someone had pressed a button and it had risen on a huge elevator for the depths of the earth. The whitewashed buildings reeked decadence. The high walls reeked privacy and a warning – enter and you will not leave except in a body bag. Guards armed with rifles patrolled both the walls and the grounds that seemed to sprawl out into the distance as far as the eye could see. They walked up to the main gate where a guard looked them both over.

"Monsieur Serpens has an appointment with Monsieur Falcone. You know how the Monsieur does not like to be kept waiting." Informed Shalamar. The guard hurriedly lifted the small bar that blocked the entrance and waved them both through. A sign on the wall called Serpens' eye, '*Nid de Faucon*.' Falcon's Nest. Serpens found that a quite apt description as he entered the nest.

Shalamar took him up the marble front steps and into the reception area of the main house, through a couple of rooms and then a long a long corridor on whose walls hung numerous oil paintings. There to impress visitors, thought Serpens, paying them little or no attention. Out into the rear courtyard where they were greeted by the sound of gunfire.

Falcone was standing just off to the right of a small group, pump action shotgun nestled in his shoulder. "Pull!" He shouted. Two clay pigeons were launched into the air. Falcone tracked them. BANG! BANG! Both clays disintegrated into two clouds of dust. He was about to shout up another pairing when he realised that Shalamar and Serpens had arrived. "Pull!" Two more clays. BANG! BANG! One died, one spun off into the distance. "Merde!" He cursed laying the weapon down on the table in front of him. He turned and greeted his guest. Shalamar bid his goodbyes and withdrew. "You like guns, Monsieur Serpens?" Serpens nodded. "What is this example then?" Tested Falcone retrieving his weapon from the table.

"Winchester Model 1912. I believe this is the sixteen gauge version. It has a six round capacity, loaded using the pump action under the barrel." He demonstrated it as he spoke. A shell was expelled from the side of the weapon and fell on the floor.

"Very good, Monsieur. Very Good." Applauded Falcone. He offered Serpens the range, Serpens stepped forward. "Be careful, Monsieur. It pulls to the left a little."

"Pull!" Shouted Serpens. BANG! BANG! Two clays were turned into dust. "Nope, seems fine to me." Serpens laid the weapon back on the table just as a woman with a baby in her arms appeared on the top step. Serpens heart missed a beat.

"Alexandre. What is all this noise? Peter is having trouble sleeping as it is."

"Apologises my dear. Just two boys playing with their toys. Monsieur Louis Serpens. Madame Molly-Beth Fallon." Serpens went forward and gently kissed Molly's outstretched hand.

"Enchanté, Madame."

"Your bracelet, Monsieur." Noted Molly. "What does it have written on it?"

"Non Est Optio Defectum."

"Non Est Optio Defectum ?" Asked Falcone.

"It's Latin, dearest Alexandre. It means failure is not an option." Replied Molly. "Where did you get that?"

"A friend."

"Foolish sentiment?" Asked Falcone.

"Family motto." Serpens gave a sly smile. A twinkle appeared in his eyes. This went unnoticed by Falcone but not by Molly, who struggled to contain herself, he could see her mind beginning to put the pieces of the jigsaw together.

"Now, my dear. Enough of this idle chit-chat. Young Peter needs his sleep." Ordered Falcone. Molly took the hint and made her excuses. Falcone waited until Molly had gone inside before continuing. "Molly-Beth is a guest of mine. She is bait for a trap I have set for her husband."

"A trap?"

"My imbecile of a son had a dispute with her husband back on the mainland and decided to kidnap her and her infant to teach her husband a lesson. Unfortunately, he couldn't have picked a worse person to antagonise."

"Really. And why is that?" Asked Serpens, his interest peaked.

"Her husband is Jonathan Fallon. Have you heard of him?"

"Fallon? Didn't he work for some secret unit assigned to the British during the war?"

"Oui. The Office of Special Projects. They cost me a considerable amount of time and money, by stopping a little venture I had going in Egypt in 1916. According to my sources, Fallon went into semi-retirement after he got married, but now my son has decided to stir up a hornet's nest." The two of them moved back into the house as the air suddenly had an added chill. In the dining room, at either end of a long table, set out to accommodate six places at each side, and one at either end, they sat at the ends momentarily sizing each other up. "What is your method of payment?"

"Diamonds are fine."

"This is acceptable to me." Falcone took out a gold plated pen and scribble something down on a piece of paper in front of him. "How much is required for your services?"

"That would depend upon how difficult the target is, and how long it takes for me to complete the assignment."

"Ah." Another note scribbled. "Do you take a down payment?"

"Expenses only."

"Ah." A nod and another note.

"You generously paid for my trip here, so we are even at the moment."

"Ah bon." Falcone rose for his chair and walked across to a small table where a decanter sat. He filled two glasses with two measures of the contents before walking across to the still seated Serpens and handed him one of the glasses. "A toast." He raised his glass and was about to speak.

"Allow me, Monsieur." Interrupted Serpens. He raised his glass. "Familia Super Omnia. Family above all."

"Agreed. Family above all." Falcone returned to his seat. "You are quite the one for your Latin quotes, Monsieur." He raised the glass again and taking another sip.

"Oui, Monsieur. I find the language invigorating, clean and almost surgical." Serpens took a sip.

"But forgive me, the language is a dead one. Non?"

"Only if you allow it to die, Monsieur."

"Ha! Agreed!" Both men raised their glasses. "To keeping things alive!" They emptied the contents. Falcone had decided for Serpens to stay in the guest chalet on the other side of the swimming pool at the back of the main house, which was round the corner from the courtyard where they first met. A guard escorted Serpens there, opened the door and then handed him the key.

Serpens closed the door and tossed his battered suitcase on the bed. He surveyed his quarters. There was a large double bed with fresh linen. A wardrobe, empty. A chest of drawers, also empty. A small bedside cabinet with a lamp on top and a single drawer. He opened it revealing some kind person had placed a King James bible.

"For some light bedtime reading." He commented as he walked over to a door and opened it. The bathroom complete with basin, lavatory and walk in shower. Serpens walked back to the bed and took out his wash bag and took it into the bathroom. He unzipped it and spilled the contents out into the sink. A blue toothbrush. Three tubes of toothpaste but only one was tooth friendly whilst the other two should have carried a government health warning – explosive health warning. Aftershave times two - one blue bottle and one green.

Shaving soap and a razor. He spaced these out on the small shelve that was just below a medium length mirror. A knock came on his room door. Serpens went and opened it. It was one of the guards carrying a pair of swimming shorts. "The Monsieur is a great one for his swimming, Monsieur. He extends the use of the pool during your stay."

"Merci." Serpens took the trunks, closed the door, and tossed them in the case. He reached into the small of his back and pulled out the automatic and waistband holster and tossed these on the bed. He closed the case and pushed it under the bed, before lying down, looking up at the ceiling cupping his hands behind his head. He closed his eyes and allowed images to float into his mind. The tall muscular and menacing Shalamar. Falcone with his silver hair. But the image that seemed to stick in the front of his thoughts was Molly standing there with the infant Peter. Had she recognised him? All the hints he had given her, surely, she had, but the plan must be carried out.

The back story that 'Sparks' had created seemed to be holding but for how long? The Colonel had pulled a lot of strings with several other agencies around the world to create Serpens and his reputation as a high grade assassin. The make-up people at the local repertory company had done wonders to change his appearance so much that even his mother would not be able to recognise him, even up close but would his body last. The beating that Lukas and his thugs had given him a couple of months before, still had not fully healed. He hoped that the slight limp he had, had gone undetected. He was snapped back to the present by another knock on the door.

"Pardon, Monsieur." It was another guard.

"Oui. What is it?" Serpens asked sleepily.

"Monsieur Falcone is hosting a small party this evening and was wondering if you could attend."

"Of course."

"Bon." The guard handed over what turned out to be a tuxedo, pressed white shirt, bowtie and pressed dark trousers. "The Monsieur has taken the liberty of supplying you with some dress shoes. He hopes you are not offended." The guard handed them over.

"No. Tell Monsieur Falcone I am honoured by his focus on detail, and I would also be honoured to attend this evening." Serpens closed the door.

At seven, Serpens showered and shaved using some of his aftershave sparingly. He put on the tuxedo plus the accessories Falcone had supplied him plus a couple of extras. His belt looked ordinary although the buckle looked a bit weird having two nodules sticking out. Pressed simultaneously released two small Indian throwing knives. He pressed the side of his suitcase and a secret panel popped open revealing a shoulder holster and a Cuthbertson CP-2 automatic pistol plus two spare magazines. He put the Colt in the compartment and closed it. The CP-2 was easier to conceal than the Colt, especially under the dressed dinner jacket Falcone had supplied.

The more Serpens thought about Falcone's methods, the more devious the man became. He put the holster over his shoulders and winced when a sharp stabbing pain went down the right hand side of his body. He flexed his shoulders allowing the straps that supported the holster to settle, moulding themselves to the contours of his upper body. The gun slipped in snuggly. The jacket completed the ensemble. The door closed behind him as he made his way round to the front of the main house, under the constant gaze of the guards. He cheekily waved at one as he walked past but with no response.

10 – The Party

The air was humid and heavy with the sound of the night. Insects making their presence felt by chirping. A cricket but that was not a subject Serpens was familiar with. The smell of burning wood and the glow of fires greeted him as he came around the corner. A multitude of guests moved backwards and forwards like a human tidal wave making progress difficult. A waiter stopped and thrust a tray of flutes into his face filled with champagne. Serpens thanked him and took one. He sipped it as he made his way through the throng of people up into the main house, where it was slightly quieter.

A string quartet played something classical in the background, just loud enough to hear but not to drown out the conversations spoken in many dialects and languages. It looked like every nation of the planet had a representative or three at the party. The Colonel and the other heads of the Intelligence Agencies would have a field day with the amount of Intel they could harvest tonight. He scanned the room. There were guards dressed as waiters.

The bulges under their jackets a dead giveaway. Guards were stationed at the top and bottom of the main staircase that would not be out of place in one of those big stage musicals that had become popular after the war. Each person that tried to go either direction on the staircase were quizzed by the guards. Any wrong answers or suspicious behaviour and you were 'escorted' to the main gate and ejected.

Suddenly there was a trumpet fanfare from somewhere that caught everybody by surprise, and this was followed by some clearing their throat. Everyone's gaze moved to the top of the stairs where a suited and booted Shalamar stood.

"Madames et Monsieurs." He announced, "your host Monsieur Alexandre Falcone and his guest Molly-Beth." A round of applause trickled up from the ground floor as Falcone and Fallon made their way down to them. Serpens watched how graceful Molly was moving and how beautiful she looked in a scarlet figure hugging dress, the sequins of which shimmered like tiny stars as each one caught the light as she moved. Falcone was dressed in a plain white suit, red tie, and dark shoes. A red carnation complemented his necktie.

Both seemed to float down the stairs only to be swarmed at the bottom by people wishing to either gain favour with Falcone or try and book a business sit down with him. The guards encircled him forming a brief protective shield before he dismissed them saying that this was a party not an assassination attempt.

Serpens had managed to find a secluded spot off to the right and used the cover of the leaves of a large yucca plant to spy on Shalamar's movements. Movements might have been an exaggeration. The man mountain stood motionless at the top of the stair surveying the festivities below with his arms crossed. He reminded Serpens of a face that had been carved into the tourist attraction Mount Rushmore, you could almost say stony faced. He giggled to himself at this thought but instantly withdrew it under a disapproving look from an older female guest. Serpens simply raised his champagne glass in her direction and took a sip then smiled. With her nose thoroughly out of joint, she waddled off after some more agreeable company.

Falcone was preoccupied with mingling, Molly managed to make her way across to where Serpens was standing.

"Are you enjoying the party Monsieur?"

"Yes, I am enjoying myself."

They moved over to the food table that had various types of delights laid out on it. Mousses. Meats. Breads and a host of other things to tempt your taste buds. Serpens handed Molly a plate and took one for himself. Then, like vultures on the open African plains, both began to scavenge from the plates, take from here, there, and everywhere. They refilled their champagne flutes and casually walked towards the doors that led out into the courtyard, all under the watchful eyes of Shalamar. The head of security summoned over one of the nearest guards saying something into his ear and pointing towards Serpens and Fallon as he did so. The guard nodded and jogged down the stairs, slowing his pace as he exited out into the courtyard.

The air was cooler now and Molly shivered. Serpens took off his jacket, revealing his shoulder holster, and draped it over her shoulders. They walked out towards the swimming pool and then sat down on one of the loungers.

"Do we know each other, Monsieur?" Asked Molly staring into Serpens pale blue eyes.

"Non, Madame. The first time I saw you was when you walked out to greet us this afternoon."

"Strange. I have the distinct feeling we have met before." She gave a nervous laugh and snorted, immediately putting the back of her hand under her nose and apologising.

"Nothing to apologise for, Madame." Something moved in the shadows that made both turn around. It was the guard Falcone had sent after them.

"Madame. Monsieur Falcone requests your presence back at the party." Molly got to her feet and took off Serpens jacket handing it back to him before leaving. Serpens got to his feet and started to follow when he was impeded from behind by the guard who pulled out his sidearm. "Monsieur Falcone said you were to remain here." The guard had his back to the pool.

"Ah." Serpens looked down at the weapon and sighed. "I wouldn't do that if I were you." He warned.

"And why not?" Asked the guard smugly.

"This is why." Serpens moved like a well-oiled machine grabbing the guard's hand and the body of the gun as he pivoted out of the line of fire. He twisted the weapon away from himself and towards the guard, prying it out of his hands. In shock, the guard just stood there. Serpens seized his opportunity and brought his right foot straight up, as if he were kicking a football catching the man between the legs, remembering his combat training, and trying to kick higher than the groin, thus retaining his balance.

The guard grabbed his lower regions, dropping to his knees which allowed Serpens to slip behind him and put him in a choke hold, by placing his right arm around his neck, grabbing his left bicep with his right hand. Serpens left hand was behind the guard's head and he squeezed his elbows together applying enough pressure on the guard's trachea to knock him unconscious.

He struggled for a moment until the lack of oxygen knocked him out. As the body went limp, Serpens looked around for somewhere to hide the body and then he was struck by a masterstroke. The swimming pool water lapping gently gave him an idea. He rolled the guard near the edge, shouted for help, and then tossed the body into the water with a splash. To add to the subterfuge, he dived in as if trying to aid the stricken man but not before throwing the gun into nearby bushes.

The splash had alerted a couple of perimeter guards who came running across to aid Serpens in pulling the guard out. Serpens pulled his sodden frame from the water and knelt over the guard. He checked for a pulse with two fingers at the side of the neck. There was not one. He tilted the head back and gave two rescue breaths before performing thirty chest compressions, pushing down hard on the man's chest, counting out aloud. He was about to repeat the procedure when the man started coughing. Serpens turned the man over on his side to allow the water he had swallowed to come out of his mouth and in case the man was about to vomit.

"What happened?" It was Shalamar.

"He did say he wanted to teach me how to Tango. He insisted on taking the lead, but I refused his advances. A lady has her standards on the first date. Pity he slipped on the tiles and ended in the pool as he was quite light on his feet, if you know what I mean?" Serpens squelched away before turning back and adding, "seven out of ten for the dive by the way." He grabbed his jacket before heading off to the guest chalet to dry off and get changed.

11 – Fallon by Any Other Name

Serpens pulled off his wet clothing, tossing the pieces on the floor of the shower. That brief explosion of exertion had taken its toll on his already weakened physique. Each movement was racked with pain. He winced and cursed as he pulled his shirt off and threw it on to the floor of the bathroom. He walked over to the mirror and looked at himself. His body was a mass of bruises thanks to the beating he had received from Lukas. His body was taking a long time to heal thanks to his lack of willingness to rest, as per Doctor's orders. He towelled himself down roughly before putting a fresh set of clothes on.

A loose fitting opens necked shirt and tanned trousers complimented by a pair of brown loafers. He was in two minds whether to return to the party. The mood, for him, had gone the minute he hit the water. But he finally talked himself into returning, grabbing a light jacket from his suitcase to cover up the shoulder-holster more than for warmth. He did a couple of shoulder circle movements to help the straps of the holster settle into position before once again, heading out.

He entered the main house through the courtyard entrance and almost immediately, Molly rushed over and asked how he was. He assured her he was fine before spotting Shalamar eyeing him up from the bottom of the stairs. Serpens tapped the back of Molly's hands reassuring her before making a beeline for the head of security.

"Don't send a boy to do a man's work." He warned as he passed Shalamar. The head of security snorted and clenched his fists as he tried to control his reaction.

"Ah, Monsieur Serpens!" Welcomed Falcone. "I believe I have to thank you for saving one of my men's lives?"

"It was nothing. The man was careless and lucky I was there." Serpens brushed off the affair.

"Nonsense. Please, come with me." Falcone headed towards the study and Serpens followed. Shalamar started to follow but stopped when Falcone shook his head. "I think I will be safe with Monsieur Serpens, Shalamar. Relax. Enjoy the party." He said, as he opened the door and ushered Serpens in. The door closed and Falcone went across to his drinks table. "Drink?"

"No thank you." Serpens declined, "I think I've had enough liquid put into me this evening." This brought a laugh from Falcone who poured himself two fingers of whisky into a glass and went over and sat behind his desk. Serpens took a chair opposite.

"Do you know why I sent for you?"

"Shalamar said you needed a problem dealt with."

"Bon." He pushed over a manila folder and Serpens opened it. It was the service record of Jonathan Fallon but curiously, no picture. "I want you to kill this man."

"But how will I know what he looks like, there's no photograph?"

"My son Lukas knows what he looks like and will point him out to you."

"Why do you want this man dead?" Serpens asked pushing the folder back across the table.

"Because he has insulted the Falcone name and in my line of business, your name is as good as your reputation."

"Why would this man come after you?" Serpens already knew the answer to his question, but he wanted Falcone to confirm it.

"Because I have his wife and child."

"Madame Fallon?"

"Oui."

"How do you know he will come?"

"Wouldn't you?" Serpens nodded. "Why all the questions, Monsieur? Does killing this man bother you?"

"No. I just want a good reason to end this man's life. I don't kill because I enjoy it. I do it because I must." Falcone looked surprised by this admission. "You have Shalamar to do your wet work allowing you to keep your distance where, when I kill, it tends to be up close and personal. So, close I can smell the target's sweat and feel their breath." He reached into his jacket and pulled out his CP-2 and pointed it at Falcone cocking the hammer.

9 2

Falcone sat a stiff as a board expecting the last thing, he would see was the flash from the barrel. "It's like just now. I have no qualms pulling the trigger right now. The built in silencer will muffle the sound so no-one will hear, but why should I? I have no reason to kill you." He slowly released the hammer and put his gun away. Falcone relaxed and took a huge gulp from his drink.

"Point taken." He said wiping the sweat from his brow with a handkerchief. "I will let you know when your target has arrived on the Island. Let me make myself clear, Monsieur Serpens, I do not want this to be linked back to me or my company. Clear?"

"Crystal."

The next morning, the ferry, Goddess of the Sea, arrived at Santa Helena for her usual drop off goods and passengers. Two of these passengers caught the eye of the local police who were permanently posted at the port to monitor the comings and goings. The first suspicious character was a man dressed in a smart suit, Panama hat, dark glasses and carrying a suitcase. The second was a woman. Slim, dark skinned and carrying an overnight bag. Both walked with intent. Both carried the air of being aware of their surroundings, the air that only special training fostered. The two police officers moved in.

"Identification." Ordered the Sergeant. The man in the suit reached into the inside pocket of his jacket and pulled out the required document handing it over. "Monsieur Fallon. Jonathan Fallon?"

"Yes. Is there a problem?"

"Non Monsieur. Are you here for business or pleasure?"

"Purely pleasure."

"How long are you staying for?"

"Just a few days. A bit of rest and recreation before heading back to the mainland."

"Pardon, Monsieur but are you armed?"

"What? What kind of question is that to ask someone who has come to visit your beautiful Island?" Protested the man in the suit.

"I am sorry, Monsieur but the Island has been put on a state of alert and I must insist you either answer my question or I will have you searched." The other officer raised his weapon. The man in the suit raised his hands just below shoulder height.

"Search me if you want, I have nothing to hide."

The Sergeant patted down the man in the suit whilst his colleague covered him with his weapon. Satisfied the man in the suit was unarmed, the sergeant handed him back his passport. "Where are you staying, Monsieur?"

"No idea. Can you recommend anywhere?"

"The Hotel Royale on the main street."

"Thank you or should I say merci." Said the man in the suit doffing his hat and moving off.

"Identification." Ordered the Sergeant again as the dark skinned woman came forward. She handed him her passport. "Miss Darla Hayes?"

"That's me, Honey."

"American?"

"Yeah."

"What is the purpose of your visit?"

"A bit of pleasure mixed with some business."

"What kind of business, Madame?"

"Problem solving." She tapped her overnight bag.

"Are you armed, Madame?"

"Nope." She opened her bag and allowed the sergeant to search it. He found a couple of changes of clothes, make-up, underwear, and a map.

"Bon. Enjoy your stay on Kalander Island, Madame." He waved her through. Hayes followed the same route as Fallon and they both turned up at the Hotel Royale. A quaint little place just off the main square. Fallon had just finished checking in when Hayes appeared behind him. He grabbed his key and went upstairs without speaking.

Hayes signed the register and did the same. Fallon drew room ten and Hayes room thirteen. She turned the key in the lock and opened the door. A musky smell greeted her nostrils as she checked the room in front of her out. A bed, chest of drawers and a hand basin with a small window off to the right. The door closed. Fallon's room was identical. The door closed.

Twenty minutes later, the telephone rang in Falcone's mansion. Shalamar answered. It was the Sergeant from the dock reporting the arrival of two suspicious passengers. The name of the female brought no reaction, but the name of the suited man was something quite different. He thanked the sergeant and then put the phone down.

"Fallon is here?" Asked Falcone astonished.

"Arrived in Santa Helena ten minutes ago. The Sergeant confirmed it with his passport."

"Why use his real name?" Falcone asked aloud. This puzzled him. A man of Fallon's reputation coming to the Island to rescue his wife and announcing the fact that he was there, did not make sense.

"What do you want me to do, Monsieur?" Asked Shalamar.

"Monitor him for the moment."

"Do I inform Monsieur Serpens?"

"What? Err...non." Falcone looked and sounded shaken by Fallon's arrival. "Keep an eye on him. If he does anything out of the ordinary, I want to know. Then we may inform our caged guard dog."

"Monsieur."

"Anything else?"

"There was another passenger on the ferry that raised suspicion..."

"Who?"

"It turned out to be nothing. Just an American tourist come to see the Island and do some business."

"I want the American watched too."

"She is just here to see the sights, Monsieur."

"What are you trying to say, Shalamar?"

"You are getting a little paranoid. The arrival of Fallon can be dealt with, Monsieur. This woman is nothing."

"Remember your place!" Snapped Falcone, "I have told you what to do. Now, carry out my instructions!"

"Monsieur." Shalamar said reluctantly.

Back at the Hotel Royale, Hayes had settled into her room and had decided to go downstairs and sit out at the front of the building at one of the numerous tables placed there. As soon as her butt hit the seat, a waitress came across and asked her if she wished to order.

"A coffee. Black." She picked up a newspaper that was lying on the table, opened it, and pretended to read. Instead, she was scanning the landscape in front of her. Watching the comings and goings of everyday life on the Island. A man with a donkey ladened with straw went by. Every so often, the man would swish a piece of stick passed the donkey's head to remind the animal who was in charge. A couple of children wheeled by on their rusty bicycles, laughing and chattering like monkeys. Hayes licked her first two fingers and turned the paper of her newspaper. Got to keep up appearances.

"Pardon Madame." Excused the waitress as she laid the coffee down on the table. Hayes looked at the steaming brown liquid in front of her. It was not in a large cup or mug like she was used to back in the States. Hell no! A dinky little European job that, after two sips, would be empty. She sighed but drank anyway.

Wow! It was like drinking neat caffeine. Her eyes almost popped out of her head as the coffee hit the back of her throat and glided down it like black lava escaping from a volcano. She attracted the waitress' attention and ordered another. She flicked the paper again and looked up to see her fellow arrival, the man in the suit, sitting opposite, also drinking, she assumed by the size of the cup, liquid caffeine. They exchange smiles. Suddenly, the man got to his feet and came over.

"Mind if I sit down?" He asked in a plum ridden English accent.

"No, please do."

"Rather a spiffing place this, isn't it?"

Spiffing? What the hell is spiffing and apart from this jerk in front of her, who uses that word? Thought Hayes. "Quaint would be how I would describe it." She finally said.

"Are you here for business or pleasure?"

"Business. You?"

"Bit of both, really." Replied the man in the suit. "The name's Fallon. Jonathan Fallon." He introduced holding out his hand.

"Hayes. Darla Hayes." They shook before withdrawing to the safety of either side of the table. The waitress returned with Hayes' refill and the man in the suit signalled for a top-up as well. "How long are you staying for Mister Fallon?"

"Johnny, please. Only a couple of days. A week at the most. I'm meeting a friend. You?"

"About a week depending upon how my assignment goes."

"Oooh! Assignment. What are you? A journalist or something?"

"Or something." Hayes sipped her coffee trying to get a read on the man opposite. She looked at her watch. "Oh my God! I'm sorry Mister Fallon. I've just realised that I've got to get ready for a meeting. If you will excuse me."

"Not at all." Said Fallon getting to his feet as the lady rose to hers. She went back into the hotel and back to her room. Once there, she opened her overnight bag and pressed two brass studs simultaneously, instantly releasing the false bottom. She lifted the false bottom out and put it on the bed. Then she turned the bag upside down allowing the contents to tumble on to the bed. There was a shoulder holster, a small automatic and a couple of files.

She married the gun and the holster before putting it on. Then she picked up the two folders, cleared a space to lie down on the bed and then lay down with the first folder held up at her face. Once she had opened the folder, the first page was a photograph of a man in his late twenties, early thirties.

She read the bio under the picture. *'Jonathan Fallon. Five foot ten with blonde hair and blue eyes. Works for the Office of Special Projects. Licence to kill. K-Twelve designation.'* Hayes cast her mind back to the man in the suit who introduced himself as Fallon then she looked back at the picture. They did not match. So, who was the suited man and why was he passing himself off as Fallon? She pondered this as she reached over and picked up the second file and opened it. It showed a picture of Alexandre Falcone, and like Fallon's one previously, it had a short bio typed underneath.

She committed both pictures to memory before putting them back in the bottom of the bag. She swung her legs over and got to her feet. Grabbed a light jacket and exited the room. She looked up and down the

99

corridor. No one. Good. She went up to the door with the number ten on it and tried the handle. The door did not give. Locked. She reached into her pocket and pulled out a black leather wallet, looked at the lock and opened the wallet to reveal various types of lock picking tools. She double checked the corridor.

Deserted, before inserting a couple of the tools, after a brief battle with the tumblers, she managed to pick the lock and silently entered the room. Hayes went to the battered suitcase and opened it. Nothing special except for two brass buttons on the side wall. Coincidence? With her curiosity fired up, she pressed the studs and low and behold, a false bottom. What the hell? There was a large automatic. A Colt '45 with a couple of spare clips. A shoulder holster and some toothpaste.

Why would he hide some toothpaste? She thought as she reached for one of the tubes then common sense kicked into play and she decided better not. She replaced everything just as she heard a key turn in the lock. Locked the case and ducked behind the door just as Fallon came into the room. He walked over to the case but stopped dead in his tracks and seemed to go into slow motion as he sniffed the air. He started to reach into his jacket but the sharp prod of an automatic in the small of his back made him raise his hands instead.

"Try anything and I won't hesitate to pull the trigger." Warned Hayes pushing him to the other side of the bed. "Who are you?"

"Jonathan Fallon."

"Bullshit!" Hayes raised her pistol.

"My name is Jericho Smithers." Smithers finally relented. "SIS?"

"Who?"

"You're with the American Secret Intelligence Service." Suggested Smithers.

"Maybe."

"Now, you wouldn't shoot your cousin from across the pond, would you?" Smithers asked slowly putting his hands down. "Why is SIS on the Island?"

"I've been assigned to stop you and your friend Fallon."

"Stop us? But why?" Hayes lowered her weapon and put it back in her holster.

"Washington doesn't want you killing one of our assets."

"Who's your asset? Surely, we're not talking about Falcone!" Said Smithers hardly believing he was even thinking of such a thing.

"Alexandre Falcone has been working for us in Africa and Europe for the last ten years. He has supplied us with vital information that has led to numerous plots being foiled both here and abroad."

"Are you stark raving bonkers!" Shouted Smithers. "The man is a cold blooded killer. We just managed to stop him turning the Arab Spring into a blood bath!"

"We know what you did, and we appreciate it."

"You appreciate it." Repeated Smithers with his hands on his hips. He put them there to stop himself from attempting to strangle Hayes.

"What else can I say? Anyway, I'm here to stop Fallon killing Falcone. Do you have any idea where he is?"

"Not a clue. My orders were to turn up on the Island and pose as Fallon. Maybe even stir up a bit of trouble."

"I think you should leave on the next ferry." Ordered Hayes heading towards the door.

"Two things that won't be happening – one. Me leaving on the next ferry…"

"And the second?"

"You stopping Fallon. Falcone has his wife and child. Good luck."

Hayes dismissed this with a brush of her hand. "If I have to use force, I will."

"How far are you willing to go, Agent?"

"What do you mean, Mister Smithers?"

"You may have to kill Fallon." Smithers suggested trying to gauge Hayes' reaction.

"If I must, I will. Killing isn't new to me." Hayes said coldly.

"It's not new to Fallon either, Agent. If you get between him and his family…"

"God help me?"

"Not even God can help you." Warned Smithers as he watched Hayes leave.

12 – Rendezvous

Serpens came out of his room and decided to take a jog around the grounds to freshen himself up. Wearing a loose fitting top, shorts and running shoes, with his CP-2 firmly secured in the waist band in the small of his back, he started to head out the back of his chalet. A couple of the guards semi waved at him as he passed, and he returned the gesture with more gusto than it had been sent. He loved to run, keeping himself in shape, the sweat staining his shirt but keeping him cool at the same time. His manly odour started to tickle his nostrils. He managed to find a rough path that headed into the small, wooded area that bordered the complex and followed it deeper into the trees.

The light went from intense to barely being able to see in front of you, as he carefully weaved in and out watching his footfall avoiding stumps of trees and the odd root that suddenly plunged itself skyward. Once through the woods, Serpens took a few minutes to find the gap in the fence he had made a couple of days previous and he squeezed through coming out on to a road that headed to a small village, some ten or so minutes away. Serpens looked around, checking to see if anyone was about. No one. Happy, he broke into a jog heading towards the village as it was time to check in.

It was part of the plan for him to check in every couple of days, failure to do so would raise a flag and hopefully, bring the cavalry riding over the brow of the hill to the rescue like they do in those comic books sold at the railway station. Cheap and nasty, Serpens agreed, but they helped wile away the boredom when travelling allowing the reader to escape into a world of heroes who would stop at nothing to rescue their family. Sounds vaguely familiar, does it not?

He walked into the village, exhausted, and covered in sweat but managed to find the local bar.

"Telephone?" He asked the busty woman behind the bar. She pointed over to the corner. Serpens thanked her and went across picking up the receiver. He gave himself a few minutes to gather his thoughts before dialling. The telephone chirped three times before a man's voice answered.

"Hello."

"The Serpent has struck." Said Serpens.

"I know. I've just had an SIS agent going mental at me. She's here to stop you, mate."

"What does SIS and Falcone have in common?"

"SIS are running Falcone. Even funding him."

"Jesus!" Serpens cursed talking the receiver away from his mouth to take a moment to think. "Does Falcone know where I am?"

104

"No. He still thinks that I'm you."

"Good. It's time I headed back before I'm missed. Stay safe, my brother."

"You, too."

Serpens replaced the telephone and was about to head back outside when the barmaid attracted his attention, waving him towards the bar.

"Police." She whispered. Serpens went back to the window and saw a Locomobile 5-passenger Sedan pull up outside with two armed policemen inside. "You can hide in the back room, Monsieur." Suggested the barmaid. Serpens refused her offer instead grabbing an apron off a peg behind the bar and draping a dirty rag over his shoulder. To complete the charade, he grabbed a mop and started to mop the floor, all the while watching the door, waiting for the two policemen to arrive. He even started to whistle, a low nonsense tune.

The officers made their way to the bar and ordered a couple of beers. The barmaid pulled the tap down slowly as she carefully filled each glass topping off each drink with an inch of foam. She placed each one in front of the officers who, arrogantly, offered no renumeration but instead swivelled on the stools, turning their backs to her.

"Monsieurs..." Serpens began using a heavy accented voice, "that is not kind. My wife works extremely hard to keep this miserable place running and you offer her no money for your drinks..." He stopped mopping and lent on the mop, his gaze staying focussed on the two men the other side of the bar. They both slammed their drinks down on the bar top causing some spillage. The barmaid picked up a rag and was about to clean it up when Serpens stopped her. "I think these kind gentlemen owe you two things…"

"And what are they?" Asked the nearest officer getting off his stool.

"An apology and the cost of your drinks." Serpens said, who was, by now, the other side of the bar. The same side as the policemen, with mop in hand, grasping the handle tighter as the first officer came towards him.

"Bullshit!" Said the officer. "I am an officer of the law, and we don't pay anything for anything on this Island." Serpens waved a finger at the officer as if he were scolding him and laughed.

"Wrong." Corrected Serpens, his smile disappeared. "You're gonna pay." And with that, he brought the mop hard straight up between the officer's legs. Before the other one could react, Serpens had swung the mop in a huge arc catching the officer on the side of the head sending him spilling over the bar. The first officer let out a scream just as Serpens turned to face him and then charged but Serpens, with the agility equal to that of a dancer, side stepped and watched as the officer smashed head long into a couple of tables. The second officer thought to go for his pistol but then grabbed the knife in his belt instead. Serpens picked up the mop and held it in both hands, his elbows bent.

The policeman lunged. Serpens blocked with one end of the mop and used the mop head ramming it into the policeman's face sending him coughing and spluttering backwards as he tried to wipe the foul-smelling liquid from his face. Serpens looked down at the first officer who was slowly beginning to stir. That lapse of concentration was costly. It allowed the second officer time to gather his wits and charge. The two bodies colliding sending both men out into the street where they landed in the dirt in a heap, the impact causing the officer to drop his knife. Serpens got slowly to his feet and took up a fighting stance, side on with one foot in front of the other, fists clenched. The first officer got to his feet and edged his way towards his opponent.

Once within range, the officer took a wild arcing swing which was easily avoided by Serpens who ducked under it, bringing his fist upwards into the man's ribs, before using the point of his left elbow into the man's back sending him crashing to the floor. There was movement in the doorway. The second officer was standing there clutching his bleeding head. He was reaching for his pistol when he suddenly lurched forward as if being hit by an unseen force, his back a mass of blood from a shotgun blast.

The barmaid walked out carrying the weapon and threw it towards Serpens who plucked it out of mid-air, turning it on the remaining officer, and discharging the remaining barrel in his general direction. The blast caught him in the chest, at first, he looked down at the wound, then up at Serpens in disbelief before dropping to his knees, where he remained as his life force drained out of him.

"Merci, Madame." Thanked Serpens handing the weapon back to the barmaid. "You could say we've cleaned up this town." Serpens said, his tongue firmly in his cheek. The quip made the barmaid smile a little.

"It's about time those bastards paid for their drinks. Every day, they get everything for free." She replaced her hair over her pretty face. Serpens went over and moved the hair aside revealing a large bruise, the kind made from a fist. At first, the barmaid flinched but then allowed him to stroke it.

"Everything for free?" Serpens repeated before replacing her hair. The barmaid nodded, tears forming in her eyes. Serpens picked up the first body under the armpits and dragged it towards their vehicle. With the barmaid's help, the corpse was dumped in the back, soon accompanied by his friend. "Don't worry, Madame. I'll deal with this."

"Merci, Monsieur."

"It's the least I can do. Remember, you never saw me or these two assholes." He searched the top corpse, produced a handful of paper money, and handed it to the barmaid. "For the damage, and their drinks."

"Understood. Merci and bon chance."

Serpens got into the driver's seat of the Locomobile, started the engine, and drove off waving to the woman as he disappeared in a cloud of dust. As he drove back, with the corpses of the officers still in the back, Serpens pondered what his next move would be. One option would be that he could dispose of both the bodies and the car in one foul stroke. True, that would solve the problem of the bodies, but he would lose the advantage of the use of the car.

The second option was to dump the bodies far enough into the woods so that it would be a while before they were discovered, hopefully giving him enough time to finish his mission. Thanks to the complexity of his predicament, his usually clear train of thought was somewhat derailed. He stopped the car and pulled out a coin. Serpens shook his head in personal disgust. This is what it had come down to – a coin toss to decide his fate. Jesus! Had things gone downhill that badly?

He flipped the coin. It spun in the air several times, almost in slow motion, before returning into the safety of Serpens hand. He turned it over on to the back of his other hand. Heads. He would dispose of everything. Tails. Just the bodies. Twenty minutes later, Serpens busied himself gathering up branches and loose leaf litter to camouflage the car. The bodies were now a distant memory but the blood stains in the back of the seat would take some explaining and he was running both out of time and daylight. He had to get back to the compound before he was missed.

The body count was rising like some cheap American Western comic book, with its cheesy story line, nasty villain and whiter than white hero. He was the dark stranger who had ridden into town and started to sort out the bad guys by any means necessary. Or at least, that was what occupied Serpens' thoughts as he ran back to the compound as fast as he could.

The alarm was raised when the Chief of Police, Captain Emile Gordona, demanded to see Falcone. A telephone call went up to the main house from the main gate. One of the guards picked up the phone and told the main gate that Falcone had still not returned from his trip to the mainland but would be expected shortly. The guard at the house took the opportunity to chastise his opposite number on the main gate for not checking the schedule sheet that was hanging up on the back of the security shack door.

The complex went into lockdown. All guards went on alert and all guests were hurriedly accounted for. The door of Serpens chalet burst off its hinges, courtesy of the boot of one of the guards, kicking it in. A couple stood just outside the doorway as two others entered scanning the room with their automatic weapons. The bed was pristine and had not been slept in. Adrenaline started to pump through their veins. Senses intensified. They searched in the wardrobe. Clothes on hangers were pushed aside. Nothing and no-one. They went and stood outside the shower/bathroom and listened. Nothing.

One was about to kick the door down, because that's what thugs tend to do in crime novels, when his partner stepped forward and turned the handle. The door swung open revealing a man's outline against the shower curtain. One of the guards went to pull it aside when Serpens head popped out with a puzzled look on his face and diluted shampoo running down his face stinging his eyes.

"What the hell's going on?" Shouted Serpens over the noise of the shower.

"Did you not hear the sirens, Monsieur?" Asked one of the guards.

110

"What? Sorry. I've got shampoo in my ears making it difficult to hear anything. What's going on? Monsieur Falcone taken a tantrum again?"

"Non, Monsieur. We are running a security check. Where have you been in the last two hours."

"Running around the perimeter."

"I need you to come to the main house immediately so that we can account for everyone."

"Now?"

"Oui."

"Errr...I'm kinda naked back here. Can I not put some clothes on first?" Serpens suggested.

"Errr...Oui." Replied the embarrassed guard shooing his partner back into the bedroom and then out the door.

Serpens waited a few moments to make sure the coast was clear before pulling back the curtain to reveal, in fact, he was still wearing his running gear and glad the guards had not pulled back the curtain any further, calling his bluff. He changed his clothes and made his way slowly up to the main house. Even though the place was going crazy, Falcone and Shalamar were obvious by their absence. Serpens wondered if someone had found the bodies of the dead officers. Surly not. He glanced at his watch. Nah! It had only been an hour or so, unless some dog walker or someone had stumbled upon them by accident.

Once everyone was assembled in the main hall, security, the guests and all the servants, a small man with glasses went and stood on the fourth step facing his 'captive' audience.

"Madames et Monsieurs," he began, "apologies for the commotion but it would seem that a couple of the local police officers have failed to return to their station. Obviously, the Chef de la Police is a trifle concerned by this and he has requested that we check where you were during this time. I am sure this won't take too long." He signalled to the other guards who then proceeded to question everyone in the room.

An hour of meticulous interrogations finally came to an end and the spectacled man thanked everyone for their assistance and patience. Making a pushing movement with his hands, he joyfully dismissed everyone but not before giving Serpens a long unsettling stare. Serpens response? A smile before turning and heading back to the guest house. The smile was one of both sarcasm and relief. For the moment, the mission was still on track. For the moment.

13 – Let's Dance

It was approaching nine in the evening when the two guards climbed into the truck and left the compound unaware that they were being followed. They were on a regular supply run to Falcone's factory on the other side of the Island, just outside the capital Santa Paulina. In the back of the truck were boxes containing the raw materials for the various products manufactured by Falcone. These included car and aeroplane parts, weapons of varying calibres and unbelievably – clothing.

Falcone had decided to branch out into the clothing design business with offices in Paris, Milan, and London. Emblazoned on the side of the truck, as with all the business outlets Falcone owned, a black falcon flying in a golden sky. They travelled with lights on whilst the car that followed did the opposite. The driver making sure to keep his distance to avoid suspicion. The journey took two hours driving at a leisurely pace.

The complex consisted of several warehouse size buildings all encompassed in an eight to ten foot high barbed wire topped fence. Like the main Falcone residence, armed guards patrolled both the perimeter and inside. Entrance was via the front gate where a machine-gun nest was positioned covering the approach road. As the truck approach, two large search lights were switched on and shone in their direction. Shalamar cast an imposing figure standing outside of the warehouses. He checked and double checked a list he had in front of him on a clipboard. Every so often, he would stop a lorry, demand the driver get out and open the back before climbing in and carrying out an inspection.

"Bon. This one is for the mainland. The next two, take them into town." He ordered climbing down and handing the driver the invoice for the cargo. Shalamar did the same for another four lorries before getting into a sedan and driving off, to join Falcone.

Meanwhile, on the hill above the complex, a car stopped, a Locomobile 5-Passenger Sedan, and the driver got out and stood on the brow looking through a pair of binoculars, noting everything that happened. A Renault flat-bed truck, its rear covered by a tarpaulin, stopped beside the guard shack, rolled down a window and passed over a clipboard. He recognised the type of truck as one of those used by the French to transport goods and supplies to and from the Front during the war. However, that was where was where is truck knowledge stopped, he did not recognise the exact make or model. The watcher from the hill guessed that on the board was

1 1 4

an invoice of what was in the truck. The guard outside the shack shone a torch over the board before handing it back, waving them through.

The watcher watched the truck disappear into the complex behind one of the many warehouses. He scanned the fence looking for a weakness, finding none, he went back to the car to rethink his plan of attack. Over the next four hours, the man in the car logged the amount of traffic coming to and from the complex. At least they were consistent, he thought as two lorries passed each other at the main gate, one entering riding high and the other exiting squashed down on the suspension.

So, he surmised, entering the lorries were empty but exiting, they were fully loaded but with what. The signage at the entrance gives little away except that it belonged to Falcone Industries. Further inspection was required, thought the man as he sat back in the car, when he heard the sound an approaching truck. He thought fast and leapt from his car and opened the bonnet. Then reached in and pulled out a torch from the glove compartment and switch it on. The truck came into view and slowly approached the car. The car driver started to wave his torch and the truck slowed to a stop. The passenger in the truck got out and started to walk towards the car, his hand on the butt of his pistol.

"What is wrong?" Asked the guard suspiciously.

"My engine just died."

The guard moved closer taking out a torch from his trouser pocket and switching it on. He moved round to the front of the car and looked over into where the engine was. He never saw or heard the car driver's CP-2 pistol fire twice. The guard fell to the ground. The car driver moved round to the blind side of the car with pistol drawn waiting for the truck's driver to react.

"Henri. Where are you?" Shouted the driver winding down his window and popping his head out, a fatal error as a slug from the CP-2 slammed into his forehead nearly taking the back of his head off in the process. The car driver opened the truck driver's side door allowing the corpse to fall to the ground. He wiped down the driver's seat before climbing aboard and starting the engine. It had been a while since he had driven a vehicle of this size, back in his army days but he hoped that it would come back to him like riding a bicycle. The gears complained as he changed them. Crunch! Crunch! But it was not long before he got the hang of it.

The sound of the second truck arriving on the road caught the guards at the complex by surprise and sent them scurrying to man the machine gun nest whilst the sergeant in charge looked down his itinerary. Nothing was due for another hour or so, so he told his men to be on alert. The vehicle pulled up and the sergeant shone his torch in the driver's face. The driver shielded his blue eyes with his hand and cursed in French. The sergeant apologised and lowered the torch.

"What is going on?" Asked the driver of the second truck.

"Who are you and what do you have in the back?" Asked the Sergeant.

"Henri is my name and I have car spares in the back. A rush job. Monsieur Falcone phoned the depot and

116

asked for these things to be brought up right away. Something about a surprise for his son."

"Henri? I don't know you."

"I am new and only arrived on the Island yesterday. Come on, man. Give the new guy a break, huh?"

"Okay, okay. Keep your hair on!" Relented the sergeant waving him through. "You're looking for warehouse thirteen." He pointed in the direction.

"Merci." Thanked the driver putting the truck into gear and heading off.

A few minutes later, the truck was parked outside warehouse thirteen. The driver got out and picked the lock. Used the chain pulley system to open the main doors before driving the truck inside. He got out and pressed the button on a small torch he had brought with him. The beam of light was not powerful enough to attract attention from those outside, but it did illuminate row upon row of wooden crates, each with the Falcone Industries logo on them. He walked over to the nearest crate, picked up a crowbar that was lying on a nearby table and opened the lid. The man shone his torch into the crate. This one, anyway, was full of glass bottles. He picked one up and unscrewed the lid. Sniffed it and then took a swig. He coughed as the alcohol caught the back of his throat. Whisky.

He walked over to another row of crates, randomly picking one and opening it. No alcohol in this one. Instead, rows of neatly packed Lee Enfield rifles. Another row and another crate. He popped the lid. More weapons, this time machine guns. The man found he was

1 1 7

seriously impressed with Falcone's enterprising ways. In public, he was the champion of the underdog preaching peace and love whilst in private, he was literally making a killing selling arms to the warring factions around the globe as well as cashing in on the fact that drinking in public was banned under the Prohibition laws.

The man would not be surprised to find out that Falcone had a string of his own private drinking dens or speak-easies scattered about the island and on the mainland too. He replaced the lids on all the crates before heading around the back of his vehicle, unlocking the tailgate, and throwing back the tarpaulin before climbing inside. He took out several tubes of what look strangely like toothpaste and placed them at various points in the back of the truck, hidden by the crates and boxes. Next, he took out a couple of time pencils and after a few seconds of mental arithmetic, pinched each pencil to allow him time to escape.

He jumped down and put the tailgate back up before exiting the warehouse. He made his way to the main gate but stopped, deciding to hide behind a couple of bushes about fifty metres from the gate and wait for the fireworks. Five minutes passed before there was a massive explosion that ripped warehouse thirteen apart sending a huge fireball up into the night sky. Alarms went off. Searchlights came on and started criss-crossing the complex. Dogs barked and men shouted. The man in the bushes used the chaos to his advantage and slipped passed the guards melting into the night.

A car was driving along the road, the occupants saw and heard the explosion making them stop by the roadside.

Both got out. One was a man in his early twenties while the other was slightly older with glasses and buck teeth. They both stood watching the sky and marvelling at the colours.

"What do you think happened, Lukas?" Asked the buck toothed man with glasses.

"Some fool was probably smoking next to a fuel dump or something." Suggested Lukas putting his hands on his hips, his face lit up by the glow from the fire. A twig snapped behind them in the forest forcing both men to turn sharply to see a man dressed all in black pointing a silenced automatic at them. The spectacled youth made a move for the safety of the car. The automatic spat death once. The youth dropped. "Do you know who I am?" Asked Lukas, distaste in every syllable. The man nodded. "Put your gun down and my father will not take any revenge upon you, I swear it." The man shook his head slowly and raised his weapon. "Wait!" The man lowers the weapon a little. His blue eyes cutting Lukas in half. "My father can make you a very rich man."

"Money means nothing to me." Hissed the man.

"Then what does?"

"Revenge."

"Revenge? For what? Who the hell are you?" Asked Lukas wrecking his brain as he tried to put the pieces of the puzzle together.

"Let me give you a hint." Offered the man. "A country lane on the mainland. A couple walking hand in hand minding their own business..." A look of horror flashed across Lukas' face. The pieces of the jigsaw had fallen into place. A light had been switched on in his mind making everything clearer.

"YOU!" He screamed raising his hands in a futile attempt to deflect the bullets, but the man did not fire. Instead, he laid the weapon down on the ground and kicked it just hard enough for it to be out of reach. Lukas looked on with a look of puzzlement.

"You took me by surprise back then when I had my family to protect. Now, I have my mind focussed on you. You and I are alone. You have no-one to come to your aid. Come on BOY! Have you got the balls to fight on your own or do you need your cronies or your father to fight your battles for you? Let's dance." The man said poking the wasp's nest that was Lukas' pride with a stick. The boy took the bait and got to his feet before bellowing like a maddened bull. He charged at the man who dodged the attack. The momentum of the attack sent Lukas crashing to the floor. The man laughed and motioned with his hands for the young man to try again. The derision only stoked the fire that burned inside Lukas, who jumped to his feet but approached more cautiously raising his fists.

The two of them circled each other like two prize fighters as they measured each other up. Lukas attacked first swinging wildly. The man countered with a right jab to the face stunning Lukas who took a couple of paces backwards, pressing his hand against his lip and looking down at the blood. Again, the man motioned for him to come forward. Up went Lukas' hands. Once within range, he lashed out with a left and a right. The first missed but the second caught the man in the ribs making him stagger a little.

Then came a whirlwind of blows from Lukas. His fists were mere blurs. The onslaught made the man cover up, his arms protecting his head as the blows rained down from all sides. Most were harmless, catching the man's arms but some managed to get through landing on the head and sides. The man retreated, giving himself some breathing room. He looked down at the automatic, wishing that he had taken the easier option and just shot this punk kid, but it was too late now.

Lukas advanced once more, buoyed up by his success. As he came into range, the man had been waiting for Lukas to make such a schoolboy error and let loose a spinning round house kick catching him on the side of the head, the blow felling the young man like a sapling breaking against the wind. Lukas lay there for a moment, dazed. The man slowly walked over and picked up the automatic before he went and stood over Lukas who looked up at him and down the barrel of the weapon. The automatic spat twice more, the bullets hitting Lukas square in the chest making him jerk as the bullets slammed into his torso.

The man fired another couple of rounds into it, just for good measure and a smidgen of pleasure. He walked over to the car and got in, started the engine, and turned the car around before driving off back the way it had come leaving Lukas' glazed eyes looking blindly up at the night sky. The blood from the four bullet holes had come together making a crimson puddle beneath the corpse.

It did not take long for news of the explosion to get back to Falcone. He was furious and demanded Shalamar found out how it had happened. News of Lukas' death came by telephone call via the Chief of Police. A farmer on his way to tend his animals in a nearby field had found the bodies. Falcone's World was starting to unravel and the first thing he thought about was Fallon's whereabouts.

"According to the police, who have been watching him since he arrived, he hasn't moved from his hotel room on the other side of the Island." Said Shalamar.

"Who else arrived on the Island with him?" Falcone asked as he struggled to hold back a mixture of anger and tears, a lethal combination.

"Several non-descript tourists and a Black woman."

"Black woman?"

"Oui. A Darla Hayes. A businesswoman here on the Island looking to expand."

"I want everything we know about this woman." Demanded Falcone, the tears had vanished to be replaced by full on rage. Revenge was now the recipe for the day and the day was getting colder. For Falcone, the stakes had been raised. If some stranger was going to attack him as if it was a real life game of poker, then he was not going to fold, he was going to call. Lukas' body was brought back to the complex on the back of a flatbed truck, covered by a tarpaulin, resting side by side with his buck toothed companion.

Falcone stood at the top of the stairs of the main house as the vehicle pulled up, standing straight, both

122

hands clasped behind his back, his eyes hidden behind a pair of dark glasses. Shalamar stood beside him. Serpens and Molly remained inside under guard in the study. They had been informed of what had happened when they had come down to breakfast.

Peter, the baby, remained upstairs under the watchful eye of Maria. A guard peeled back the tarp. The bodies had been laid on wooden pallets and it took four guards for each to carefully lift them down from the truck. Falcone had ordered them to take the corpses into a small shack off from the main complex.

It was air conditioned, hence cooler. Each group slowly and respectfully walked towards the building. You may be wondering at this point, where Lukas' mother / Falcone's wife, was at this sad occasion? She was killed by one of Falcone's rivals several years ago in a failed assassination attempt.

Needless to say, this rival is no longer with us. In fact, the authorities found what was left of him inside the stomach of a Great White Shark a local sports fisherman had managed to catch several weeks later. It is widely known how slow the digestive system of the shark is. The puzzling thing was his rival's body was that it was missing its eyes. This still baffles the international law enforcement authorities to this day. Satisfied, Falcone turned and went inside to his office closing the door behind him. A knock came at the door.

"Enter."

It was Shalamar. "I have that update for you, Monsieur."

"Update?"

"Darla Hayes. The woman who arrived with Fallon on the ferry."

"Ah, Oui."

"She used to work for Kitty O'Connell…"

"O'Connell. How is that name familiar to me?"

"She owns the 'Kit-Kat' Club franchise. She has several clubs internationally. It was rumoured she worked for the British during the last war."

"How does this Darla Hayes fit into the equation?" Asked Falcone lighting a cigarette and taking a drag from it.

"Hayes worked for her during the war before disappearing off the radar only to pop up on the Island a couple of days ago."

"I need you to contact our friend and find out more about this Hayes."

"But Monsieur!" Protested Shalamar. "Our friend has instructed us that he is not to be contacted unless it is an emergency. He was most sincere about that."

"My son is lying on a piece of wood only a few hundred metres away!" Yelled Falcone, "I think we could say this constitutes an emergency!"

Meanwhile, at the Hotel Royale, Smithers was sitting on his bed drinking a coffee when a knock came at his door. He walked over and was halfway through turning the handle when the door burst open sending him sprawling to the ground. He instinctively scrambled over to the bed where his forty-five was lying only to find himself pushed face first to the floor by a boot to the middle of his back. Lying there, spread eagle, Smithers felt both undignified and vulnerable in equal measures. A hand, a female hand, reached over and picked up the forty-five releasing the pressure on Smithers' back allowing him to turn over.

"What the bloody hell did you think you were doing?" Raged Hayes pointing her automatic at Smithers.

"If I knew what you were talking about, I would answer the question."

"You blew up one of Falcone's factories last night and killed his son as well eliminating anyone who could identify Fallon and them torpedoing your little ruse."

"Firstly, I have no idea what you're talking about and secondly, I spent all of last night doing as ordered – staying visible for the local plods across the street." He slowly got to his feet and walked over to the window pulling back the curtain just enough for them to look out on the street below. He pointed over to the small café across the street where two men in dark suits sat facing the Hotel. "They take it in turns to watch my movements. If I go for a walk, one is always a few steps behind me. They're methods are amateurish but effective." Hayes lowered her gun.

"Then who killed Lukas Falcone?"

"Who do you think?"

"Fallon?" Smithers nodded. "But why?"

"Jesus! And they call the organisation you work for, the Intelligence Service!" Smithers threw his arm up in despair. "As you rightly said, Agent, Lukas could identify him, and this put him and his family at risk. You could

1 2 5

also put it down to a little side order of revenge on Fallon's part too." He walked over and picked up his coffee and sat down on the end of the bed. "By the way, you know who I am, but I believe we haven't been properly introduced."

"My name is Hayes. Darla Hayes." She extended a hand of 'friendship' which Smithers took, squeezed lightly and then let go.

"Pleased to meet you, Miss Hayes."

"What do we do next?" She asked joining him on the bed.

"That depends on Fallon. We just can't go rushing in."

"Agreed."

"What back-up do you have?"

"Several agents ready to come to the Island on a moment's notice. I've also got a naval destroyer with marines on board ready to assist off the coast if needed."

"Jesus! You Yanks like to do things big, don't you?" Commented Smithers.

Over the next forty minutes, Hayes, and Smithers exchange notes with the American telling him that the SIS had long since suspected Falcone was being funded by a rogue section of their agency but could not prove it or find out who was actually running Falcone. That was the main reason she was on the island with the secondary mission of stopping Fallon. The SIS needed Falcone to testify against his former bosses which meant, they needed him alive and did not need some revenge crazed Brit going off half cocked.

1 2 6

Smithers, in turn, told Hayes about their plan to infiltrate Falcone's business from within and rescue Molly-Beth and the child. Despite Hayes' reservations, she took the executive decision to allow the plan to run its course and to be there to mop up afterwards. She reluctantly agreed not to inform her superiors in case the suspected leak was in the chain of command.

14 – Our Masters Aren't Pleased

The clock was striking noon when the car pulled up in the car park. It was the only vehicle there. Inside, Falcone and Shalamar sat in the back whilst a couple of guards took up the front seats. Falcone looked at his watch. This was the first time Shalamar had seen his boss nervous. Falcone had always been a man of control. He was not one of these anonymous figure heads you hear about in most companies who have their pictures plastered on every wall in their office buildings and come out every so often to be aired and to show face. Not Falcone. He led from the front and had no problem with getting his hands dirty. Whether it was in the cut-throat world of high finance or dealing with a treacherous employee, Falcone was there, in person.

The head of security understood he could not fathom the depths of emotion Falcone was feeling at the moment but seeing his boss look at his watch for a second time in as many minutes both disturbed and worried him.

"He is late." Falcone said tapping his watch.

"He will be here, Monsieur." Reassured Shalamar.

Just then, another car came into the car park and parked several metres away from them but facing them. Headlights flashed which was a waste of time really being that it was in the middle of the day, but this is standard spy craft one-oh-one. Shalamar was the first to get out and he made his way around to open the door for Falcone. The two guards also got out and were carrying sub-machine guns, the latest models from Falcone Industries. As Falcone keeps saying to his workforce, it does not hurt to advertise.

Doors of the other car opened. Two armed men in the front and two men dressed in raincoats and dark glasses from the rear. The two men from the rear were dressed similarly but looked totally different. The one on the right was heavier set with a beard and bald head. The one on the left was younger looking. Muscular with brown hair and unlike his companion, clean shaven and a chiselled jaw line. The four 'passengers' moved to no-man's land between the two vehicles whilst the guards remained back watching.

"Why did you call?" Asked the heavy set man.

"We have a problem." Replied Falcone.

"Oh." The heavy set man said with a hint of surprise in his voice.

"Darla Hayes."

"Ah." The heavy set man was a man of very few words.

"Why is she on my Island?"

"Your Island?" Repeated chiselled jaw. "May I remind you, Falcone..."

"Monsieur Falcone!" Corrected Shalamar.

"May I remind you, MONSIEUR Falcone..." Said chiselled jaw emphasising the 'monsieur' part, "that we paid for your luxurious lifestyle so that you could freely move within the circles that you currently do so that you can supply us with relevant information."

"Who is this little puppy who does not know his place?" Asked a disgusted Falcone.

"This is Brad Williams and he's Darla Hayes' section chief." Replied the heavy set man.

"Then may I suggest he keeps his mouth closed until he is spoken to." Suggested Falcone. Williams opened his mouth to reply but the heavy set man stopped him with a shake of his head.

"Walk with me." Asked the heavy set man. Falcone raised his hand to stop Shalamar following as the two men moved away from the group. The two men went to the edge of the car park which overlooked the river and stood there talking, sometimes their actions were very animated, voices raised on occasion allowing the group to catch snippets of conversation.

After half an hour of discussion and waiting, the two men returned to the respective groups and vehicles and parted without a word. The drive back to the yacht was an uncomfortable one for Shalamar because he was used to his boss confiding in him, but Falcone just sat their grinding his teeth and every so often punching the arm

130

rest, like a schoolboy would after being dragged up in front of the school's headmaster and scolded for something he did not do. They got to the yacht and went on board.

Falcone went straight to his cabin while Shalamar ordered the crew to cast off and head back to the Island. For the whole three hour journey, Falcone remained in his cabin and had left strict instructions not to be disturbed. Things could be heard being thrown from within. Cursing both in French and English.

As the yacht drew alongside the quay at his own private mooring, Falcone sent word for Shalamar to join him in his stateroom which ran the whole of the top deck. Shalamar knocked on the door and entered. Falcone was sitting on one of three large, padded couches with his legs crossed and a glass of whisky in his hand.

"Please, my friend, sit." He motioned to one of the other couches. Shalamar sat down on the edge. "Let me apologise for my behaviour the past few hours..." Falcone began. Shalamar, upon entering the room, had noticed that his boss' demeanour had changed from the silent, brooding man post discussion to a more relaxed version. "Our masters in the SIS aren't happy that we have the Fallon woman and her child and are demanding we release them. Pressure from someone called Forrester, I believe. This man Forrester sounds quite formidable. Like myself in my younger days..." Falcone smiled and took a drink.

"Are we going to do as they say, Monsieur?"

"It is too late for that, Mon ami. Someone has killed my son and that someone must pay." A cold glint

131

suddenly appeared in Falcone's eyes. "Send word ahead that I want everyone's rooms searched at the main house."

"Even the Fallon woman's?"

"Oui. It would appear we have a snake in the grass, mon ami, and it is my intention to find it."

15 – The Snake is Revealed

A knock at the door of the guest house. After a few moments, the door opened, and Serpens appeared wearing a loose fitting shirt, shorts, and sandals. His blonde hair combed back over his head; his blue eyes tinted red due to the shampoo violation.

"Please follow us, Monsieur." Instructed one of the guards as they proceeded to walk to the main house, like rats following the pied piper of Hamelin. Serpens tried to lighten the mood by adding a couple of skips but soon ceased under the glare from the guards. They entered through Serpens favourite exit, the courtyard and made their way to the study. The door was open which was strange as it was standing orders from Falcone that it remained closed. Standing at the desk was Falcone who turned as Serpens entered. Inside, Shalamar stood to the right of the doorway and Gordona was sitting on one of the couches, sweating profusely, a drink of whisky, in his hand to calm his shot nerves.

"We have a problem." Falcone spoke finally as Shalamar closed the door and then stood at the door facing them, arms folded. "My son was killed two days ago by an unknown assassin, one of my factories was also blown up on the same night and now I am told two policemen are missing…" Serpens went over to the drinks table and calmly helped himself to two fingers worth of whisky before sitting down on another couch, watching, and listening to Falcone intently. "I asked a friend to perform an autopsy on my son and do you want to know what the results were?" He looked around the room at his captive audience. He was about to speak when he was interrupted by a knock at the door.

Shalamar opened the door to reveal Molly standing there, flanked by two armed guards. "Come in, my dear." Molly was almost pushed into the room and the door closed again. "Sit beside Monsieur Serpens, if you would." Molly, confused, did as she was told. "Where was I?"

"The results of the autopsy, Monsieur." Reminded Shalamar folding his arms again and puffing out his chest.

"Ah, Oui. My friend found that my son had been shot four times by a weapon that uses an unusual calibre of bullet. He said that there is only one organisation that uses such a weapon – the Office of Special Projects!" A look of stunned shock and a sharp intake of breath followed this revelation. Someone in the room faked the reaction. "I have checked with my backers, and they informed me that the weapon concerned is called the

Cuthbertson CP-2. Now, this weapon has a distinctive look..." Falcone moved behind his desk to face his audience. "And the people gathered here, apart from Madame Fallon, are all armed." Falcone pulled open a drawer and brought out a large gold plated automatic, laying it on the table. "Shalamar." The head of security walked forward, reached into his jacket, and brought out a similar large automatic, laying it down on the table beside the other one. "Gordona."

"What is this rubbish?" Complained the Police Chief. "You suspect me of killing your son and two of my own men? Absurd!" He got to his feet and started for the door. Shalamar put one of his massive arms around the policeman's neck and with his other hand reached down for his holster pulling out a revolver. The two joined men turned to face Falcone.

Falcone gave a short sharp nod. Shalamar tightened his strangle hold around the policeman's neck, who struggled, arms flailing, hands clawing, as his life's breath was squeezed out of him and then - SNAP! The Chief's body went limp. His neck was snapped like a dry twig. Molly screamed and hid her face in her hands. Serpens looked on coldly, expressionless. The door of the study burst open and two armed guards stood there, their weapons drawn.

"Dispose of the trash." Ordered Falcone coldly. What happened next took everyone by surprise. Serpens slowly got to his feet with a wry smile on his face and reached to the small of his back bringing out his automatic, laying it on the table and then sitting back

135

down. The automatic was a CP-2. He put his hands on his knees and looked straight at Falcone who looked back astonished. Shalamar was out of the room assisting the guards dispose of Gordona, so it was just Falcone, Molly, and Serpens in the room. Everything went into slow motion as Serpens jumped to his feet and raced across to the table just as Falcone started to reach down for his weapon. BANG! BANG! BANG!

Falcone looked down at his chest where the three bullet holes were, then looked up at Serpens, who stood there unarmed, and then across at Molly who stood there with a small automatic still smoking in her hand. Falcone dropped to the floor, face down. Serpens turned and took the gun from Molly.

"Who are you?" She asked, tears running down her face.

"Some people call me Louis Serpens...."

"Serpens? Wait!" Molly said, wiping her face with the back of her hand. It was as if a lightbulb had gone on in her head and she had just figured it out. "It means 'snake' in Latin. Like the phrase 'snake in the grass,' someone who is not to be trusted. The bracelet. Non Est Optio Defectum..."

"Failure is not an option..." Translated Serpens.

"But that's the motto of my..."

"Family."

"Jonathan?"

"Yes, darling. It's me."

"But how?" Molly asked still in shock.

"Amazing what some theatrical make-up and some hair dye can do." Said Fallon as they embraced, giving each other a lingering kiss, which was interrupted by someone clapping. They stopped and turned back into the room. It was the 'corpse' of Falcone applauding them and then he picked up his weapon. Fallon and Molly turned back to the door only to have their exit blocked by an armed Shalamar and several guards.

"Monsieur Serpens?" Falcone paused for a moment as he pondered the name and then it hit him, "Monsieur Snake?" Some of those present would think that this was a light bulb moment for Falcone, but no one dared to say it out loud. "You are a superb shot, Madame. Bravo!" He applauded Molly and then motioned for them to sit. Shalamar took the small gun from Fallon and added a small shove as an incentive.

"How?" Asked Molly referring to Falcone's amazing resurrection from the dead.

"My suit is made from a special weave. We call it the Lazarus weave. It is bullet and knife proof. Something my organisation has been working on for my friends the Americans." He walked over to Molly, putting the barrel of his weapon against her cheek and slowly running it up and down. Fallon tried to get up but was force back down by Shalamar's vice like grip on his shoulders. Molly let out as small whimper. A cruel pencil thin smile appeared on Falcone's face as he repeated the gesture a couple more times before composing himself and turning his attention to Fallon. "So, you are the famous Jonathan Fallon. The man who foiled my plans in Egypt. Who cost me millions."

"I see my reputation precedes me." Quipped Fallon. His jest was rewarded by a double squeeze on the pressure points in his shoulders making him wince with pain. He looked up at Shalamar, who just grinned a satisfied grin back at him.

"I have a special place for people who get in my way, Monsieur Fallon…It's called Lac des Âmes."

"Lake of Souls." Said Fallon.

"Your French has been excellent, Monsieur, as has been your little ruse as Monsieur Serpens. Bravo! However, like all good things, it must end." Shalamar stepped forward and manhandled them to their feet. "Take them to the lake."

"What about my son?" Screamed Molly.

"He will be raised as my own. A replacement if you will." Falcone waved his index finger in the direction of the door. Molly managed to break free and lunged at Falcone who countered by slapping her to the ground. Fallon moved forward and was floored by the butt of a rifle to the head. "Such passion." Falcone said in admiration as he walked triumphantly across to the drinks table and poured himself a celebratory glass. He turned and raised his drink to his fallen foe as they were carried away, then he laughed, a long and hearty laugh before taking a long and enjoyable drink from his glass. He had won but his heart was heavy with the loss of his son. The Fallons were going to pay with their dearest blood whilst the product of their union would become the heir to the Falcone dynasty. Would he tell the young Peter of his background? Only time would tell.

16 – Rescue

Fallon was awakened from his forced slumber by screaming. He opened his eyes and blinked, allowing his eyes to focus. The screaming was coming from Molly. She was pleading for him to wake up. He looked over at her and saw she was sitting on a bench and the bench was moving. No, the whole room was moving. It took him a few seconds to realise that he was in the back of a vehicle, a truck, heading where only the driver knows. Suddenly, the vehicle stopped. There was the sound of men's voices at the front of the truck and then the tail gate was dropped, and the tarpaulin thrown back. Two guards climbed in and manhandled Fallon to his feet. Another helped Molly down before Fallon was tossed to the ground. All was quiet except for the lapping of water nearby. Fallon got to his feet with the help of his wife, it was then he realised his hands were tied behind his back, Molly's tied at the front. The guards raised their weapons and ushered them forward towards the sound of the water.

"What's happening, Jonathan?" Asked Molly, fear evident in her voice.

"It would appear we've outlived our usefulness, Darling."

They were pushed through some bushes and came out into a large clearing containing the main feature of Kalander Island – Lac des âmes. The guards positioned their captives facing them with their backs to the lake. Fallon and Molly closed their eyes and waited for the gunshots to ring out. Instead, they heard a mixture of engines and hooves. Another sound floated towards them. A familiar sound but a musical one. Philip Souza's 'Stars and Stripes.' The guards looked at each other with a mixture of puzzlement and panic. A booming voice came from the bushes.

"United States Marines! Stay where you are!" The bushes disintegrated as two large trucks mowed them down and a group of about twenty men on horseback followed close behind, all armed with automatic weapons. A large machine gun on the cab of the first truck was pointed at the guards manned by, of all people, Smithers. "Put your weapons on the ground or we will open fire!" Boomed the voice over the music which was being piped out through a speaker attached to the second truck. As the guards laid down their guns, other soldiers piled out the back of the two trucks, the ones on horseback had, by now, surrounded the guards who raised their hands in surrender. Smithers jumped down from the truck and rushed over, quickly freeing Molly and then Fallon.

"How?" Asked Fallon.

"You missed your appointed rendezvous, and I got curious, so I rushed over to the compound just in time to see you bundled into the back of the trucks." Explained Smithers.

"Where did you get the calvary?"

"That would be thanks to me, Major Fallon." Said Hayes, "Darla Hayes. Special Intelligence Service." They shook. Immersed in the moment, Fallon and the others had failed to notice that the driver of the truck that brought them to the lake was now levelling his automatic at Fallon's head. His finger tightened on the trigger, and he slowed his breathing as not to miss the shot. The hammer slowly moved back and then.... BLAM! And splash as his lifeless body hit the water some five feet away, such was the impact of the round that hit him square in the chest. Everyone looked in the direction where the shot had come from, to see Gerald Cuthbertson sitting on his bottom with his legs spread eagled, a large pistol with smoke still coming out of the barrel in his hands.

"Where did you get that cannon, Sparks?" Asked Fallon walking over and extending a hand to help the man up, which he duly took still trying to get his breath back after being winded by the recoil.

"Allow me to introduce the CP-3 BG or CP-Big Gun."

"Impressive." Admired Hayes.

"Do you not think CP3-BG a bit of a mouthful, old boy?" Asked Smithers.

"I totally agree. That's why I prefer to call it by the name the Colonel gave it. CP-3 Magnum. It carries six

141

point-three-five-seven slugs, but I think it's better in someone's hands who knows how to use it." He passed it to Fallon.

"We need to get back to the compound." Reminded Molly.

"Not a problem. Hop on board." Invited one of the marines as they were hauled aboard the second truck which reversed back through the bushes before doing a hard one eighty and sped off down the road. The sound of gun fire greeted them as they approached the compound.

Another group of marines, supported by SIS agents were already there and engaged in a firefight with Falcone's men. Smithers popped up behind the machine gun on top of the cabin and proceeded to fire a short burst in the direction of the main gate, killing four guards instantly, as the truck smashed through the gate. Everyone piled out the back firing their weapons at any enemy target. Marines and guards alike fell under the hail of lead.

"I'll go after Shalamar." Shouted Molly. "You go for Peter." Fallon waved that he understood, and the couple separated.

On the field at the back of the compound, the Armstrong Whitworth bomber idled away as Shalamar loaded up the small compartment behind the pilot with a small briefcase loaded with bonds and money from Falcone's safe. There was enough there to keep both men comfortable for the rest of their lives in some country that does not extradite to any of the allied countries. Molly came running round the back of the house and heard the plane's engine, following it to the field.

She drew her weapon, a CP-2, and made her way cautiously towards the plane. But why would Falcone leave the plane unguarded she thought looking around. She took off a small bag that one of the marines had given her containing several grenades. Molly was about to pull one of the pins and toss the bag into the rear cockpit when a huge hand grabbed her neck from behind and threw her like a rag doll against the fuselage, winding her. She looked up to see the hulking shape of Shalamar.

"Now, I kill the bitch!" He hissed pulling a large knife from his waistband, the sunlight dancing on the blade, as he moved towards her. She slowly got to her feet, wiping a trickle of blood away from the side of her mouth and taking up a defensive pose with fists clenched and hands raised. Shalamar laughed but the smile soon disappeared when one of Molly's fists unclenched as she reached down for the CP-2 that had been knocked from her grasp during the attack. She raised the gun slowly, cocking the hammer.

"Don't call me bitch!" She pulled the trigger. BANG! The shot caught Shalamar in the shoulder, the impact making him lurch to the side but not before he let loose with his knife. The blade buried itself in Molly's leg and she collapsed to the ground grabbing the wounded limb. Shalamar laughed again as he climbed into the pilot's seat and gunned the engine. He looked back for Falcone. He was nowhere to be seen, so he pushed the throttle forward and the plane started to gather speed. Molly pulled herself painfully to her feet and waved at him as the plane took off.

143

Puzzled by Molly's gesture, Shalamar banked the plane around and headed back over her. She made another gesture and shouted above the engine noise. "I left you a little present in the back." She pointed and held up a small circular metal object and dangled it on her index finger. It was a pin from one of the grenades. While Shalamar was concentrating on getting the plane up to speed, Molly had managed to throw the bag of explosives in the rear cockpit. Shalamar looked back into the back of the plane just before it erupted into a huge fireball. The force of the blast was so intense that it knocked Molly off her feet.

While Molly was battling Shalamar, Fallon had entered the main house with his new Magnum in hand. "Falcone. Where are you?" He yelled, searching a couple of rooms, and kicking the door down of another.

"I am here." Fallon turned to see Falcone standing on the landing above him, holding a screaming Peter by one leg dangling him over the edge. Fallon started to climb the stairs. "Stay where you are, K-Twelve or I drop your son." Fallon froze.

"What do you want?"

"Safe passage to my plane and no interference when we try to leave."

"And if I disagree?"

"Simple. We see if your son can fly." He moved his arm further out to underline his threat. Fallon raised his hands.

"Okay, you win."

"Drop the cannon and kick it away."

Fallon dropped the magnum and kicked it off to the side. Just then, the finale of the fight outside reached its climax. The explosion caught Falcone off-guard giving Fallon a split second window to reach around his back and pull out the CP-2. BANG! The first shot caught Falcone in the shoulder with no effect. He laughed. "Have you forgotten I am wearing the Lazarus suit. You can't kill me while I'm wearing it."

"I hadn't forgotten." Said Fallon through gritted teeth, "that was merely a distraction." He fired again. BANG! This time, the bullet hit Falcone in the middle of his forehead. A trickle of blood ran down his nose. His eyes rolled back, and he fell forward releasing his grip on the infant. Everything seemed to go into ultra-slow motion like you see with the action replays at modern day televised football matches. In one movement, Fallon dropped the CP-2 and stretched out his arms like a goalkeeper frantically trying to keep the opponent's shot from going in his goal. He dived forward using every ounce of strength he could conjure.

Smithers and Hayes burst into the main hall to see the corpse of Falcone spread eagle over what used to be a table, which had smashed when his body landed on it. And there, sitting in one of those cushioned plush chairs sat Fallon cradling Peter in his arms. He looked up at them.

"You, okay?" Asked Hayes putting away her pistol. Fallon nodded. "Falcone?" She motioned over to the body.

"Yeah. A bad case of lead poisoning." There was a slight pause before the three of them burst out laughing.

"What's all the hilarity?" Asked a female voice from the doorway. It was Molly leaning heavily on the shoulder of a burly marine sergeant.

"Falcone is dead." Said Fallon, "Shalamar?"

"I blew his mind." Molly said hobbling over beside Fallon and looking down on her son who, even with all the noise, was fast asleep. She smiled. "Sleep well, my Prince." And bent down to kiss him on the forehead. Fallon handed Peter over to her and the small group went out into the courtyard where the Marines were busy mopping up the last of Falcone's men.

"What about the plane?" Asked Fallon.

"Like Falcone's dreams, it went all to pieces." Replied Molly.

17 – Rise Like a Phoenix from the Ashes

Smoke and flames rose from the burning vehicles turning the scene like something out of Dante's Inferno. The smell of bodies and burning rubber made even the strongest stomach turn. The odd crack of gunfire in the distance sent the message that some of Falcone's men had not given up the fight. Hayes looked over at Fallon.

"Go."

Hayes smiled and grabbed a couple of nearby Marines before climbing on board a truck. "See ya around Cowboy."

"Count on it." Replied Fallon putting his arm around Molly.

"How will you get home? Wanna lift?"

"Nope. I've got that covered." Fallon smiled and looked at Molly who looked back at him mystified.

"Fair enough." The truck engine roared as the vehicle moved off through the gates.

Fallon escorted Molly, Peter, and Smithers around to the side of the building where Falcone kept his most treasure possessions – his cars. He picked one, a Rolls-Royce Silver Ghost, and they got in. Now, I know I said earlier, that Falcone had a liking for American automobiles, but when it came to his own personal way of travelling, he liked to travel in style, hence the leaning towards the crème de la crème of motoring, you could not beat the British.

The journey only took five minutes and it terminated at the private dock where Falcone's yacht bobbed up and down. Molly let out a giggle of delight as she and Peter went aboard. With Falcone's men either fighting the Marines, captured or in hiding, there was no-one around to offer any resistance. Fallon and Smithers joined them on the yacht.

"I've got this, Sir." Said Smithers picking up a Captain's hat that was hanging on the small steering wheel. Fallon nodded and took his family downstairs and into the master bedroom. He walked over and checked out an adjoining door, opening it to find that it was a smaller bedroom. Molly placed Peter in the centre of the bed, draping a light blanket over the sleeping infant, before quietly closing the door but leaving it slightly ajar. Fallon lay on his back with his hands clasped behind his head looking up at the ceiling. She joined him laying her head on his chest, his left arm snaking around her waist.

"I knew you would come." Molly whispered stretching up and kissing him on the cheek.

"Did you ever doubt it, Darling?"

"Never."

"How so?"

"Failure is not an option." She smiled as she got on top of him, they kissed long and passionately.

Hours later, a telephone rang in an office in Madrid. A man in a white suit with a carnation in the buttonhole, picked it up. A male voice on the other end informed him of Falcone's demise. He swore in Spanish and then hung up the receiver.

"Bad news?" Asked Brad Williams as he puffed on a large cigar and leaning back in a wicker chair.

"Falcone is dead. It would seem our friend Fallon is more resourceful than we first credited him."

"With Falcone dead, they cannot link him to me or us. So why are you worried?"

The man in the suit walked out through the french doors that opened out onto a balcony. He looked out at the vista in front of him before answering. "Our business interests could be affected by what has just happened, and that worries me and our backers. They are powerful people who are done with the bureaucratic way things are done by the World's governments. Setenta Ocho will rise from the ashes of the Falcone incident." He turned and came back into the room, picking up his glass and raising it in a toast. "Setenta Ocho!"

"Setenta Ocho!" Toasted Williams, standing. Williams sat back down. In some ways, he was glad Falcone was dead. As he had stated openly, with the death all links to the American Secret Intelligence Service had been severed like a gangrene infested limb. Its backing of Falcone and

149

his business Empire had been buried in the mists of time. Cleansed. Williams raised his glass once more and gave a silent salute before downing what was left.

The white suited man went back out on to the balcony and raised his glass skyward. "Like a Phoenix rising from the ashes, Setenta Ocho will return and crush all those that oppose it. Jonathan Fallon. Your days are numbered. Count them wisely my friend. One day we will meet, and it will be you against me. Mano a mano."

Williams raised his hand like a schoolboy trying to attract the attention of his teacher. The man in the white suit looked at him and raised a quizzical eyebrow. "Why is our organisation called Setenta Ocho? I've always wondered that." He said as he twiddled his large black ring around on his finger. The number seventy-eight glinting as the light caught it.

"That is a very good question, Mister Williams. According to legend, the number seventy-eight could refer to the year our great organisation was formed. Eighteen Seventy-Eight. Another theory goes that it refers to the number of original members that signed our charter but there is no definitive answer. All I know is that it is an honour to serve." The man in the suit walked back out onto the balcony taking his glass with him, leaving Williams to ponder his explanation. He took a drink and then looked down at the street watching the people below going about their business unaware evil was watching them from upon high.

A new era was about to begin for Setenta Ocho whilst a new hero has been born into the Fallon Dynasty, ready to take his rightful place as a legend.

150

"Yes, a new era would herald the rise of a new hero...." Repeated Fallon and then he snorted, the noise waking him from this slumber. It had gotten dark outside. How long had he been asleep? He took out his pocket watch from his waistcoat pocket and looked at it. It was nearly ten o'clock. He got slowly out of his chair and stretched, yawning as he did so. His neck was in knots. He lent his head to one side then the other, forwards and backwards, as he tried to loosen it off. It was slightly better. His half empty glass of Scotch was calling his name, whispering sweet nothings in his ear in a vain attempt for attention. For a moment, he did consider finishing it but decided on the lure of his nice comfortable bed waiting for him upstairs.

He left the study and stood at the bottom of the stairs looking up at the portrait of his younger self that stared back at him. The Fallon motto emblazoned on the plaque underneath the painting – Non Est Optio Defectum. Failure is not an Option. Words that he had tried to live by in his life with the Office of Special Projects since he had joined them in the middle of the Great War.

"Yeah, a new hero would take up the mantel of the Fallon family in the storm that was brewing on the horizon at the end of the thirties but at what cost?" He found himself asking an empty room. He looked around to see if anyone had seen or heard him talking to himself. He was alone, thankfully. Smithers had long since turned in. His tongue clicked on the roof of his mouth, as was his custom when he thought wistfully, shook his head, and then slowly, and purposefully walked up the stairs taking each step with a measured and paced step.

"A new hero...." He muttered to himself once more as he closed his bedroom door quietly behind himself.

The End

Don't miss the next instalment...

ROBYN SMYTHE

Fallon III

THE GATHERING STORM

Coming Soon...